"Wanna come •

"I can't." She wanted to, though. Oh, how she wanted to. "I, uh...

"And o... do that...

Ignori... "I didn... for put... sofa."

"We both did." He leaned on the door again. "Guess the day was longer than we realized."

Davia nodded. "Well, I'll let you get back to sleep."

"Are you serious?" Though he didn't explain his comment, she saw it his eyes. He was awake now. And feasting on the sight of her. He rose to his full height and gave her a curious smile... ...door wider. "Come in, D...

Again, he... ...brown, sleek and... ...uld almost feel... ...their desire to crawl across...

"Kale, I can't.

Dear Reader,

Thanks bunches for diving into my latest Kimani Romance title. If you follow me on social media then you know I'm a serious movie fanatic! You could say that *Silver Screen Romance* is somewhat of a testament to the movie lover in me—toss in our stunning hero Kale Asante and I'm… well…in love.

The unexpected attraction between Kale and our heroine, Davia Sands, offers romance, mystery and another of my faves—winter weather. Yeah, I know that snow can be a pain but Kale and Davia find lots to do in the sleepy Midwestern town where they've inherited, of all things, a movie theater. I crafted *Silver Screen Romance* while imagining you curled up with your favorite hot beverage and peeking into the lives of this gorgeous, sexy couple. Here's hoping the steam is to your liking.

Email your thoughts to altonya@lovealtonya.com.

Love,

Al

Silver Screen ROMANCE

AlTonya Washington

HARLEQUIN® KIMANI™ ROMANCE

Recycling programs
for this product may
not exist in your area.

ISBN-13: 978-0-373-86483-6

Silver Screen Romance

HARLEQUIN®
www.Harlequin.com

Printed in U.S.A.

AlTonya Washington has been a romance novelist for over eleven years. She's been nominated for numerous awards and has won two RT Reviewers' Choice Awards for her novels *Finding Love Again* and *His Texas Touch*. AlTonya lives in North Carolina and works as a college reference librarian. This author wears many hats, but being a mom is her favorite job.

Books by AlTonya Washington

Harlequin Kimani Romance

As Good as the First Time
Every Chance I Get
Private Melody
Pleasure After Hours
Texas Love Song
His Texas Touch
Provocative Territory
Provocative Passion
Trust In Us
Indulge Me Tonight
Embrace My Heart
Treasure My Heart
Provocative Attraction
Silver Screen Romance

Visit the Author Profile page at
Harlequin.com for more titles.

For those who enjoy their love stories in print and…on-screen.

Chapter 1

Miami, Florida

"Where?" A hint of laughter mingled with the element of sincere bewilderment in Kale Asante's question. His voice was rich, its tone possessing a warmth that was equally displayed in his liquid-chocolate gaze.

Kale's lawyer, Felton Eames, looked to be on the verge of laughter himself. "Mullins, Iowa," Felton said once he'd spared a second glance toward the documents in front of him. The sheet was one of several spilling from the charcoal-gray briefcase lying open on the black-walnut coffee table in his client's den.

Kale appeared to be considering the information while he rubbed the tip of an index finger across the long line of one sleek brow. Amusement came through that time in the form of a chuckle before more words followed. "I honestly can't recall ever visiting the place or knowing anyone who has."

Felton nodded while rubbing his fingers through the cap of salt-and-pepper waves covering his head. "I didn't think you had," he sighed. He grabbed another of the documents that languished over the open edge of his case and passed it to Kale. "But it looks like your late uncle did."

San Francisco, California

"Where?" Intrigue was the resulting emotion when Davia Sands heard the name Mullins, Iowa. Her clear, hazel eyes sparkled more effervescently than normal while she observed her business attorney.

Bess Gaither merely continued to swivel in the burgundy scoop chair she occupied, smiling over her client's reaction.

Davia turned her bright, wide stare toward the document that outlined the news Bess had come to deliver that afternoon. "How could I own land in Iowa and not know about it?" Unmistakable bewilderment had her voice in its clutches.

Bess ceased her swiveling and left the chair to top off her coffee at the bar cart on the deck where she and Davia conversed. Though the day had been a surprisingly comfortable one and rich, late-afternoon sunlight doused the deck, a chill still carried on the early January wind.

"Specifically speaking…" Bess said, pausing as if to add a dramatic flair while she filled her coffee mug to the brim with the aromatic blend. "You don't own land, but a building. Or, from what I understand, what's left of one."

"Okay…" Davia rebundled herself into the afghan that helped the sweatpants and long-sleeved tee keep her warm against the breezy day. "So how'd I come to own a building—or what's left of one?"

"Seems you've got Miss Glory to thank for that." Bess used the smug manner she put in place whenever she was about to eviscerate or merely stun someone at a negotiating table.

Davia sat a little straighter on the lounge she occupied. Bewilderment had her expression in its clutches that time. "What's my late aunt got to do with—" she checked the document again "—Mullins, Iowa?"

Bess prepped her coffee, adding sugar and cream to suit her taste. "If you bother to actually read that page I gave you, you'll see that Miss Glory spent quite a bit of time there during the early forties. She inherited the building from a Chase Waverly when he passed away in 1956."

Davia regarded the sheet in hand with greater interest. "That can't be right." Her voice held a quiet, considering tone, as though she were attempting to convince herself. "I've never heard anything about this. I don't think even my mom and dad know."

Gloria Sands was the older sister of Davia's father. The woman had been Davia's favorite relative across the whole of either of her parents' extremely large families.

"A woman's life is a trove of secrets." Bess's sigh held the unmistakable air of playful mystery. She gave a theatrical twirl away from the bar cart with her steaming mug of coffee still firm in her grip.

"What sort of *mystery* could my aunt have been involved in in Iowa?"

Bess inhaled the fragrant steam drifting off the mug. "Guess you'll find out on Wednesday."

"What's Wednesday?" Davia's tone was absent at best. She was still aptly reviewing the document Bess had provided.

"The day you meet with the Mullins town council."

Davia dragged her eyes up from the page and simply gaped at her lawyer.

"Are you serious?" Kale pinned his lawyer with an unwavering look and could see all too clearly that the man was completely *not* joking. "What the hell do I have to meet with the town council for?"

Felton rested his elbows on his knees and conducted a mini thumb war between them. "Seems that after over sixty years the town of Mullins has finally had enough of looking at that piece of land you've come into. They find it to be an eyesore that's driving down the property value in that area of town. *That*," Felton said and brought an end to the thumb war, "and there's talk of a developer wanting the land to put some overpriced artsy shops on."

Felton spread his hands and shrugged. "The town is calling this its good-faith effort at reaching out to the rightful owners. I think everyone who had a hand in this was all pretty surprised that there were any. At least, they *acted* surprised. I can't get a straight answer on how it was overlooked that your uncle and Ms. Sands inherited this property over two decades ago."

Kale rubbed at his head, crowned by a crop of light brown waves. "You got any info on that place? Demographics? Economic info?"

Felton's tanned, hard-lined face softened with an easy smile. "I know what you're getting at and the answer is no. Mullins wouldn't be suited to any of the kinds of projects you like to sink your teeth into."

Kale gave his lawyer a begrudging look. "It's good to know you're worth what I pay you." He shook his head while softly laughing before somberness took hold of his voice and expression. "We should see if there's any truth to this rumor of a developer. If so, I want to find him and make an offer. Unload the property while I can."

"Kale—"

"If the developer's a myth, find out who I need to make an offer to in Mullins. I'm pretty sure my uncle wouldn't have minded."

"Kale. You can't do that, man."

It was rare that Kale heard those words directed at him. While he'd been raised to be humble and appreciative, it was at times difficult to express those qualities. So often, the very nature of his business made the showcasing of such qualities...unnecessary.

At any rate, Kale worked to be a fair-dealing, fair-minded kind of guy. A successful industrialist didn't become a successful industrialist without earning a respected name.

Still, in spite of all that fairness, humbleness and appreciativeness, Kale struggled with—hell, he *despised*—

being told that he couldn't do something. In all honesty, he was doing his best to work on that.

Kale could tell from the look on his attorney's face that the man was getting a kick out of witnessing him in the throes of dealing with that which he despised. Determinedly, he put in place a patient air that was quite obviously a fake.

"So why can't I do that?" Kale approved of how level his voice sounded.

Felton nodded toward the page he'd given his client. "You own the land. Someone else owns what's built on it."

"Okay, just so we're clear, are you laughing because this is good news or because you're pissed? I can never tell with you."

Davia left her lounge, dregs of laughter still tumbling past the perfect bow that was her mouth. "For future reference, this is my pissed laugh," she told Bess.

Bess nodded as though she were mentally filing away the information. "Does that mean you know Kale Asante?"

"Know *of* him." The words felt like grit on Davia's tongue. She persevered to deliver more explanation as she went inside.

"The land development world is a small one, once you reach a certain level." Davia studied the view of the bay from her desk, hoping its calming effects would drench her. "Kale Asante's name has its own penthouse address there."

Davia hated the pinched tone she heard in her voice. She wasn't exactly jealous of Kale Asante's accomplishments. After all, *her* name held residence along the same address strip as Kale's, if for different expertise.

As a cultivator of undervalued properties, Davia had been schooled in the art of recognizing diamonds in the rough from an early age. A product of her aunt's tutelage, Davia had become a force in the realm of quaint movie theaters. Truth be told, she and Kale Asante orbited different quadrants of the same hemisphere.

There had only been one time when those quadrants had intersected. Regrettably, it had been time enough for Davia to form a none-too-complimentary impression of the well-known industrialist.

"Of course you know her," Felton drawled, completely unsurprised as he repacked his briefcase.

"I know *of* her," Kale clarified with an easy grin. "I've never met her. What?" he queried. Something in Felton's resulting chuckle had him very curious.

Felton shuffled through his case again and took from it a black folder that he handed to his client.

A long, low whistle drifted past the beckoning curve of Kale's mouth when he saw the 8x10 color glossy inside. "You are definitely worth every cent I pay you," he said, his gaze repeatedly scanning the photo that captured the woman's image from head to toe.

"This is very true." Felton raised a hand. "Kale Asante, meet Davia Sands."

Kale understood the man's amusement. The fact that he of all people had never met the woman in the photo was wrong in so many ways.

"Can't believe you never bothered to find out what

she looked like," Felton noted absently once he returned to packing his case.

Kale's deep-set dark brown eyes scanned Davia's image again. "Our last…interaction wasn't under the friendliest circumstances," he said. "It was a rather abstract interaction at best."

"Business is rarely friendly, my man." Felton smiled through a grimace.

"Mmm." Kale took another moment to skim the additional information in the folder before he closed it. "That's especially true when your adversary thinks you cheated a client to close the deal before she died."

Felton sealed his case as he looked up at Kale. "Martella Friedman."

Nodding, Kale shut the folder but set it on an end table instead of returning it to his lawyer.

"Davia Sands was in the running for the theater that inspired the lobby for my last multiplex. Seems I bought it right out from under her."

Groaning, Felton flopped back against the black suede sofa he occupied and dug the heels of his hands into his eyes. "So…Davia Sands hates your guts and you're now fifty-fifty owners of an inherited property."

Kale settled against the back of an opposing sofa. Folding his arms over a well-defined chest, he appreciated the view of the Atlantic beyond his balcony. "That about sums it up." He sighed.

"So, should I tell Sully to get the jet gassed up for Iowa?" Felton asked, still massaging his eyes.

Kale took the black folder from the end table, thumbed through it again. "Actually…I've got another stop in mind."

Chapter 2

"So, how about we set the meeting with Sorrells and his guys for the twenty-sixth? Yeah, I'm not thrilled about it, either, but I may be out of town for the next few days, maybe longer…" Davia frowned over the contents of a folder as she entered the lobby in reading mode. Meanwhile, her crew chief's voice filled the earpiece of the headset she sported.

Davia smiled, having caught her receptionist's frantic wave across the room. Laughing softly, she turned her focus back to her call with Curtis Wilkes.

"Curt? I need to go, but I'll be in touch before I leave. Hopefully by then I'll have more details about this trip."

Davia took another minute to wrap up the call with Curtis. Her receptionist was almost out of her chair as she waved toward the bank of windows overlooking the famed Golden Gate Bridge in the distance.

"Leslie, what is it?"

"Davia, it's Kale Asante."

Davia allowed uncharacteristic surprise to illuminate her face as she stepped forward to greet the man who, until that time, she'd only seen via camera stills and promotional photos. She was offering her hand to accept his shake when he began to speak.

"Ms. Sands, it's a pleasure."

"Same," Davia sighed, a little pleased she'd been able to respond. He had, without argument, taken her completely off guard.

"I know we don't have an appointment," Kale was saying, "but I'd appreciate you making time to see me."

Davia managed a nod, still somewhat off-kilter by the man's unexpected arrival. Absently, she tugged off her headpiece and caused her boyishly cropped locks to fall in disarray around her dark, fine-boned face.

Kale reciprocated the nod while taking inventory of the woman. Deftly, he assessed the features he hadn't been able to fully appreciate during his study of the file his lawyer had provided him the night before.

His warm, appealing stare was fixed on every move she made from dragging her short hair back from her face to fingering the thick black plastic band of the headset she held. He didn't know how long she'd been calling to him before he realized he'd been all but drinking her in with his gaze.

"Sorry about that." Quietly, Kale cleared his throat and gave a quick shake of his head before meeting her eyes once more. "Would you mind repeating that?"

"Would you like to go to my office?" Davia asked obligingly, her tone just as quiet.

Kale hesitated before answering. Of course, going to her office was the logical move. They needed to talk, but to hell with him believing he'd be able to focus on a damn thing alone in a room with her. A silent, stony voice interrupted his thoughts to remind him that she hated his guts.

Kale nodded, the gesture accompanied by a fluid smile. "That sounds good."

"Davia? Your assistant's not at her desk," Leslie pointed out, her blue eyes bright with interest. "Is there anything I could get for Mr. Asante?" A few beats passed and then she shook her head. "And for you, too, Davia."

"I'm fine." Davia arched a brow in Kale's direction. "Mr. Asante?"

Kale sent an adoring smile toward the receptionist. "I'm good, Leslie, but thank you."

"Yeah, thank you, Leslie." Davia spared the woman a knowing look and wondered if Kale Asante could sense how very much her receptionist wanted to see to his needs.

"If you change your mind, I've got a bar in my office," Davia said as she led the way.

"Uh, thank you." Kale blinked away from where his gaze had drifted. He was pleased he'd managed the response before Davia Sands grew suspicious of his silence and turned to find that he was more focused on the way she moved beneath her clothes than on her offer for a drink.

Davia didn't seem any the wiser and was showing Kale into her office suite a few moments later. The room had the remarkable ability to pull his eyes away from his hostess's beckoning figure. He summoned a whistle while surveying the vast space of the corner digs and all it held. All the comforts of home.

"Tell me you don't sleep here." His rich voice held the distinct chord of wonder.

"All right." Davia allowed her quiet to do the talking. When Kale laughed, she joined in.

"I put in a lot of long hours." Her slight shrug sent a ripple through the fabric of the olive-green shirt dress that drew the eye to the stunning length of her legs. "After a while, it gets hard to focus, so it helps having my favorite things around to help me unwind."

"Favorite things, huh?" Kale smiled over the phrase while running the back of his hand along one lever of the elliptical machine he stood closest to.

Davia proffered a knowing smile. "Necessary."

Kale had to bite his tongue before he found himself telling her she must spend a great deal of time on that which she found "necessary." Her body, though willowy, appeared toned with subtle yet tempting curves. His palms heated with the desire to see if his eyes were in any way deceiving him. Upon first glance, he wagered she'd break if he held her firmly enough.

Aside from the exercise equipment, the office boasted a cozy entertainment area. The spot was complete with floor-to-ceiling bookshelves filled to capacity with books and an array of DVDs and CDs. The overstuffed recliner in the far corner held a pillow and a fleece blanket and looked to be the perfect nook for a lengthy snooze.

Davia Sands's work digs were almost an exact replica of his own. Somehow, though, he didn't think she would appreciate knowing they had anything more in common.

"So…Mullins, Iowa," he said.

"Mullins, Iowa," Davia repeated. "Have you ever been there?" she asked.

"Not yet. I decided to drop in and meet you first."

"Why's that?" Davia asked while heading to her desk where she set down the headset she'd used.

"A few reasons." Kale followed her across the room.

Davia took a seat along the front edge of her white oak desk. Raising her hands, she silently encouraged him to continue.

"I've been told that Mullins isn't the sort of place that'd be suitable for one of my properties." Kale eased a hand beneath his suit coat to slide it into a trouser pocket.

Davia gave a cool smile. "Lavish, expansive, expensive," she said.

"My reputation precedes me, I see." Kale steeled himself from grimacing. He'd immediately regretted his choice of words. He had hoped to save the discussion of his reputation—or rather, *her* perception of his reputation—for later.

Davia didn't appear on edge. Moreover, she seemed amused, as though enjoying a joke she wasn't quite ready to share the punch line for.

"Yes, Mr. Asante, your reputation has definitely preceded you."

Kale acknowledged her thinly veiled insinuation with a faint nod. "I came to see you, hoping we could've discussed plans for you to buy me out."

"Could have?"

Kale nodded once more. That time he shared with Davia an approving smile. "You're a thoughtful listener," he commended.

Davia tilted her head to acknowledge his accuracy. "It pays to hear what the other person is really trying to say. If people did more of that, maybe a lot of misunderstandings could be avoided."

"I'll have to remember that." Kale watched Davia as if he'd discovered some additional facet to her appearance that had him newly intrigued.

Davia looked as though her interest had risen a notch, as well. "So you were coming to discuss plans to sell your part of the property but you've…changed your mind?"

"I have."

"Something I said?"

Davia's thinly veiled insinuation was met with a grin that broadened as he spoke.

"It is, actually." Kale could see the wave of shock freeze her exquisite features.

There was no going back now. The conversation he'd just as soon put off until…well, never, would soon be under way. Before that, he thought a little clarification of his earlier comment was in order.

"It's about what I overheard you say when you walked in earlier."

Davia drew into herself, attempting to rewind her thoughts.

"You said you'd planned to be out of town for the next few days, maybe longer," Kale supplied.

"Yeah. That…that's right." Davia silently admitted

she was stumped, having no clue where the conversation was headed.

"May I assume you meant out of town in Mullins?"

"You may." Davia folded her arms over her chest. Her curiosity was through the roof.

Kale lowered his head as if deeply focused on the unraveling of a mystery. "Is it also safe to assume that you're not thinking about selling your part of the property?"

"Well, I... No." Davia blinked, once again stumped. "No, I don't think I could sell it, Mr. Asante."

He shook his head. "Just Kale. Kale's fine." Actually, most everyone who knew him referred to him by his first initial but—and he would only admit it to himself—he very much wanted to hear her say his name.

Davia obliged. "Kale. I just don't think I could sell it."

The hint of a frown began to darken his dreamily crafted face. "Why? Did your lawyer say something that turned you against it?"

Davia remained cool. "Well, no, it…it's a gift. Or it was. A gift from my aunt—something she would've wanted me to have." She left her perch on the desk and moved to the floor-to-ceiling windows that provided a spectacular late-evening view of the Bay area.

"I have my aunt to thank for my career." Davia's voice held a soft, faraway tone that hinted of some nostalgic air. "She could've done anything with that property had she known about it. That it's come to me… that it belonged to her…that means something to me."

Kale had moved to the windows. He stroked his jaw, a contemplative look taking over his features. "Yeah…

I see what you mean," he murmured while he looked out over the evening skies, as well.

Davia turned, resting her shoulder against one of the tall windows. She watched him, trying to decipher the path of his thoughts.

Kale didn't keep her in the dark for long. "Why do you think your aunt and my uncle left it to us? Why are we just finding out about it now?"

Davia let a quiet sigh escape. The question was nothing new to her. "I asked my lawyer the same thing. She doesn't think it was so much *left* to us as it was an asset that was somehow overlooked when the estates were settled after their deaths." She stood back to fix him with a kind smile.

"I don't know how it went with your uncle, but my aunt never married, never had kids. Everything she had went to me. We, um, we were close like that."

"Same with me and my uncle." Kale turned, putting his back against the window. "My mom's got four brothers, but she and Uncle Bry—Bryant Leak was his name—were closest in age and he was the one I bonded the closest with." He smiled, the nostalgic air having claimed him then, as well.

"I got my love of the movies from my uncle." Kale grinned, resting his head back on the window. His grin took on a heightened definition when he heard Davia laugh.

"I've got my aunt to thank for that," she said. "That's why all my projects are theaters."

"Same here," Kale concurred. "So what do you think caught their eye in Mullins, Iowa, that made them buy it?"

Davia shrugged. "Did your uncle ever mention the

place?" She strolled back to her desk, resting against the edge once more.

"Not a peep." Kale pushed off from the window. "I never heard of it before talking to my lawyer yesterday."

"Yeah, me, either." Davia sighed. "I guess it's worth it to at least go and see what's out there. Then I can decide where to go from there."

"Well, just so you know, I don't plan to fight over it—whatever it is. I mean to accept whatever offer you make me and I only plan to accept it from you."

Davia closed her mouth once she'd finally realized it was hanging open. Easing off the desk, she reclaimed the chair behind it. "Why would you do something like that?" she managed to ask after a lengthy pause. "From what I've heard, there's some developer already interested in the area. You're sure to get a pretty penny from selling to them. Why give me the option?"

Kale claimed the spot Davia had abandoned along the edge of her desk. "A few reasons."

She laughed, swiveling her chair a bit. "You still haven't shared all the reasons you came to see me."

"That's right." He gave a playful wince that simply intensified the dreamy appeal of his creamy, chocolate-doused features. "Like I said, I came to see you about selling the place." His expression turned more serious and his eyes darkened. "I also came to see if you were as incredible to look at in person as you were in the file photo my lawyer gave to me."

Davia felt her heart make an unexpected and frantic shimmy into the back of her throat.

"And…I came to talk to you about Martella Friedman."

Davia's heart stumbled into a suddenly upset stomach. She sighed. "And just when we were getting along so well."

Chapter 3

"So your generous offer is motivated by guilt."

"No."

Davia regarded him through narrowed eyes. "Then why are we discussing Martella Friedman?"

"Because you're misinformed about what went on there."

"I see… Misinformed that you seduced her business out from under her."

His laughter was brief yet full of genuine humor.

"Very misinformed," he insisted.

Davia resented the feel of her mouth tightening but she couldn't help it. "Kale, this all went down years ago, you know? Why offer an explanation about it now?"

"We've never been business partners before."

"We aren't business partners now."

He gave a slight nod. "Closest we've ever come."

"Not quite." Davia left her chair and returned to stare out over her view again.

"I was there the day her creditors came calling."

Davia rounded on him, her expression a mixture of amazement and suspicion. "I think you mean her predators." The clarification sounded hard as stone.

Kale seemed satisfied. "Looks like we've at least got a *little* information in common."

Davia turned to the windows again. She didn't want to cry for her friend in front of this man—this stranger. "So, what happened? How is it you came to own Tella's theater?"

Kale smoothed his fist inside his palm. "I think you know I don't own it now."

"But you did. Explain that."

Kale took a seat in Davia's desk chair, appreciating the decadent peach suede encasing every inch of the furnishing. "I was there that day for inspiration for an annex I was building on one of my multiplexes. I was looking for something inviting, quaint… Martella's theater had what I wanted…what I was hoping to recreate in my spot. That's all. We weren't in business, Davia." He waited, hoping she would turn so that he could judge her expression. There, he hoped to find just a little understanding. When she didn't turn, he continued.

"I was on my way out for the day. I was in town for a few days and had planned to come back to make a few notes before I left for Miami. I went by her office to let her know that I was going and I overheard her inside with her…creditors. It didn't take much to get the gist of what was up. The place wasn't open yet for business.

I guess they figured they'd caught her there alone." He paused as the memory overtook him.

"I was about to go in to break *their* legs before they could break hers—which was what they were threatening."

By then Davia had turned from the window. Her gaze was rapt with interest as she absorbed the story. "Did you think you could take them?" She tried to ease her jitters by teasing.

Kale smirked a little. "Not before I got in the office." He shrugged. "Then I was pretty sure I could, but I also heard her telling them she'd have all the money with interest by the following Monday. I heard the figure, went in there and made a big deal about the place being just what I wanted. Then I made an offer. Forty K over what she needed."

He leaned forward, bracing his elbows on his knees.

"I pretended to be surprised when I noticed her friends," he went on. "I told her I was ready to transfer money as soon as I saw the paperwork and such. Told her I'd be back with my people later in the week." He smirked again, the gesture carrying lethal intent.

"The garbage in there with her said it wouldn't be necessary, that they were on their way out. They left and she broke down, told me everything. The gambling—how deep she was in and to how many people. I wound up padding a hundred K onto what she owed to the guys in her office."

While Kale talked, Davia sat in a chair in front of her desk. "But what happened? How—?"

"I made the mistake of returning with one hundred and seventy-five thousand in cash."

Davia closed her eyes and hung her head. "Tella..." she whispered, lamenting her friend.

"Even still, she wanted everything by the book. She would've refused the money otherwise. She didn't want it to look like a handout." Kale shook his head. "I had the papers in hand the next day." He left the desk chair. Fist clenched, he slowly paced the area behind it.

"I was an idiot," he said, his rich voice carrying across the room, "charging in there like that without bothering to think. I should've known when I heard how much she was in for that she had a serious problem. I should've anticipated that she'd—"

"You couldn't have anticipated that." Davia scooted toward the edge of her chair. "She didn't want help. Not the kind we were trying to give her. Not the help she really needed." She slumped back then and pinched the bridge of her nose.

"I'd been talking to her about selling the theater to me. She wouldn't even consider taking my money outright when I offered—and it looked like she was even going to turn down my offer to buy it." Davia let out a soft, cold laugh. "Had I made the kind of gesture you did—padding the offer like that—she probably wouldn't have accepted that, either."

Kale's fierce expression had softened as he'd listened. "Sometimes it's easier to accept help from strangers than friends. How long have you guys been close?" He came over to take the empty chair beside her.

"Since college." Davia gave a shaky smile. "When I found out her family was in the theater business, my aunt went with me for a weekend visit." She closed her eyes in appreciation of the memory. "Such an amazing place…"

"Very amazing," Kale said.

"That weekend we saw *Bram Stoker's Dracula*." She smiled as she remembered.

"Coppola's?" Kale queried.

She nodded. "This was several years after the movie originally premiered. Tella's family was known for doing theme weekends. That weekend all the films were dedicated to the infamous Count and it rained the whole time. The theater had such a cozy old-world style. It was the perfect venue to screen a period piece like that, not to mention all the others we saw. It was a fun trip. My aunt had the best time getting to know Tella's family and I had the best time getting to know Tella a little better."

Again, Davia felt tears pressuring for release. Again, she willed them back before she turned to Kale. "Why didn't you ever say what really happened instead of letting folks believe you—?"

"Because letting them believe that bile was better than the true filth of it. At least, what I saw as being filth."

"You tried to help."

Kale snorted. "I've wondered about that over the years. Wondered if it was all about me trying to make myself feel better in the moment. Like I'd come to the rescue and been the kind of gentleman my uncle always swore a *real* man should aspire to be."

He rolled his eyes. "That was someone I had no interest in being. Women always gave me what I wanted without me ever having to play the gentleman's role."

"Gave? Past tense?"

Thoughtful listener indeed, Kale mused. "They still do. I guess somewhere along the way I started having a problem with it." Suddenly he laughed. The gesture held no amusement. "Had I thought more about what Martella really needed—"

The phone's shrill buzz filled the room and Davia didn't know whether to celebrate or curse the interruption. Moreover, she didn't know what to do with the sudden empathy she was feeling for a man she'd practically loathed for the past several years.

Pushing up from the chair, she leaned over the desk to grab the phone. It was her assistant. "Hey, Maggie."

"Davia, sorry for the interruption." Maggie Phelps's airy voice breezed through the receiver. "Leslie told me you were in there with Kale Asante. Is he as sweet and sexy as she claims?"

In her own sly manner, Davia surveyed her guest, who had turned to stare out at the view. "A definite yes to the second and a possible yes to the first."

"Well, I'm sorry to take you away from your meeting, but I figured this concerned you both."

"How so?"

"I've got an Estelle Waverly on the line. She's calling from Mullins, Iowa."

"A call from Mullins?" Davia said for Kale's benefit.

He turned, curiosity alive in the chocolaty pools of his deep stare.

"Put it through, Maggie," Davia instructed and then put the phone on speaker. She waited a beat before greeting the caller. "Mrs. Waverly? This is Davia Sands. I'm here with Kale Asante."

"Oh, that's great! I'm so glad I caught you both together." The woman's voice surged into the room.

Kale reclaimed his preferred spot at the edge of Davia's desk. "Mrs. Waverly, is there a problem?" he asked.

"Will the two of you be able to make it to the town council meeting? Did your attorneys tell you about it?" the woman asked.

Kale and Davia traded looks.

"We know about it," Davia said.

"Are we expected to attend?" Kale picked up on the anxious quality in the woman's voice.

Estelle Waverly chortled. "It depends on who you ask. My husband's uncle—Chase Waverly—was the original owner of the property. The story of how you two came to own it is an involved one best saved for when you arrive. Can we count on you to be here?"

"You've got us curious, Mrs. Waverly," Davia replied. "I can't help but say that curiosity does include a fair amount of suspicion."

"Sounds like this is about more than Ms. Sands and I coming to take a look at property we've inherited," Kale tacked on.

Estelle Waverly released another of her delicate laughs. "Oh, Mr. Asante, it's definitely about more than that. Please tell me you'll be here for the meeting."

Kale and Davia exchanged another look before she accepted the invite. "We'll be there, Mrs. Waverly."

"Fantastic! Thank you both so much!" The smile was evident in the woman's voice. "There's no need to make hotel arrangements," she was saying. "My husband and I own the town bed-and-breakfast, and your rooms are already prepared. Pack warmly, it's January and this is Iowa, after all." She sighed. "Our apologies for this all sounding so unorthodox, but I think you'll have a better understanding of things once we've had the chance to speak in person. Thank you both again."

The connection broke. Kale and Davia stared at the dead phone for several silent seconds.

"What is it we're considering exactly?" Davia queried finally.

Kale was shaking his head slowly. "Guess we'll find out when we get to Mullins."

"Why do I get the feeling we're going to be there for more than a few days?" Davia tapped her nails along the top of her desk.

Kale grinned. "At least we know our rooms are ready."

Davia wasn't feeling so at ease. "Did you come to San Francisco on your own, Kale, or is your lawyer here?"

"I'm alone. I hadn't actually planned to go any farther."

"Well, it looks like we're both heading out there without anyone to watch our backs, then. I kind of left my lawyer hanging on whether I wanted her along on this first trip. Now I'm regretting I didn't ask her to join me."

Kale nodded. "You know, some might argue if I claim I'm not a sexist, but I'm perfectly fine with you watching my back."

Davia had to smile.

"I won't take offense if you don't feel comfortable saying the same, but I'll watch your back, anyway."

"I'd appreciate that." Her smile held. "So why do

you think Estelle Waverly wouldn't say more over the phone?" Though she honestly wanted to hear his answer, Davia was more interested in avoiding answers about where she stood on the subject of his true involvement with Martella Friedman.

Kale got to his feet. "At least she told us our coming there is about more than just looking at property we inherited."

"I feel like I should be exercising some sense of precaution, but my curiosity is winning out."

"Mine, too." Kale was heading for the bar but paused midstep to gesture toward it instead. "That offer for a drink still stand?" he asked.

Davia gave a consenting wave and began to pace the perimeter of her office. Moments later she was dialing her assistant.

"Maggie, have you printed my tickets to Iowa yet?" Davia felt a hand at her elbow while Maggie's voice filled her ear.

"Have her cancel the tickets," Kale was saying.

Frowning, Davia slowly tuned into Maggie telling her the task was next on her list. "Hey, Mag, hold off on that, will you? I'll call you back in a sec." She hung up and looked at Kale. "Cancel the tickets?"

He gave her a look of phony discomfort. "Would telling you that I own a jet make you hate me even more?"

"I already know you own a jet. That fact is more than obvious."

"Hell." Kale looked decidedly uncomfortable as he released her elbow. "How?"

Davia's laughter made a boisterous entry. "Surely the guy who envisioned the era of the luxury multiplex rates such perks!" Her eyes narrowed to fix him with a lightly discerning look. "Do trappings like that disturb you?"

"They do when I'm trying to gain the approval of someone who's already got me in the doghouse. And since the cat's out of the bag," he continued before Davia could refute his doghouse claim, "*and* since we're going to the same place, the least I could do is give you a lift."

As her sense of precaution and treading carefully had pretty much abandoned her, Davia didn't see the harm in going all-in. "Lift accepted. Thanks."

Kale nodded his satisfaction and tilted his head toward the desk where a beer mug waited next to a frosted bottle of the brew. "Enjoy your drink. I'll see you later."

"Aren't you having something?" she called, realizing he was leaving.

"I've got it stocked on the jet. I'll have one later."

Davia glanced at the bottle, noticing it was her own label. "How—?"

"My attorney's file was very detailed." Kale's eyes sparkled as he enjoyed her surprise. "It's a good product, Davia. You should be proud that you're a partner in that brewery. See you later."

"And I suppose you already know where I live?"

Hand on the office doorknob, Kale paused and turned to her. "Like I said, my attorney's file was very detailed. I'll see you, Davia."

The door closed at his back just as Davia released the breath she hadn't realized she'd been holding.

Chapter 4

Davia headed home to pack more. The turn of the discussion with Estelle Waverly had clearly indicated that more than a three-day stay would be required. But why?

Realizing her thoughts had rendered her immovable inside her walk-in closet, Davia shook herself. She pulled a few more garments from the rack that held everything from fisherman's sweaters to ankle-length cardigans and shearling coats.

She had a pretty good idea that her questions pertaining to the Mullins affair would be answered soon enough. What she wasn't sure of was whether her questions pertaining to Kale Asante would be answered. Her conversation with him had taken an intriguing turn, as well, she recalled.

What he'd had to say about Martella…was it really

true? She had spent so long living under a completely different version of the truth. That version of the truth felt good, it felt safe. Yes, that truth was like a warm blanket, because the more time she could spend despising Kale Asante for Martella, the less time she had to despise herself for not doing more to help her dearest friend. Still, she hadn't been able to shake the man's explanation. Something about what he'd shared stuck with her. When he'd spoken, she'd felt a tug of sincerity in his eyes.

She couldn't stop the snicker that tickled the back of her throat. A tug from the sincerity in his eyes? While she wouldn't claim Kale Asante wasn't sincere, that element hadn't been at all responsible for the definite tug she'd felt in his presence.

Earlier, she'd been amused by her receptionist's clearly dazed demeanor around Kale. While he'd been exceptionally polite to Leslie, Davia had the sense the man was both accustomed to and appreciative of the reactions he drew from the women fortunate enough to make his acquaintance.

Davia tossed another sweater into the case a bit more forcefully than necessary. She cringed over her selection of the word *fortunate* but…hell, she was alone. She could admit she'd felt fortunate indeed to have been given the opportunity to look upon such a specimen like Kale Asante.

His looks were assuredly a study in patient craftsmanship. It was rare that she met a man who managed to make her feel dwarfed by his height when she was decked out in heels, for which she had what had to be an unhealthy obsession. With her feet encased in a chic, strappy pair like the ones she wore, her height could top out at a whopping six-two.

Not that such things mattered. The men Davia met were usually business-related instead of personal. She hadn't been thinking of Kale Asante in a business sense...

Davia shook herself again, selected more sweaters from the closet and dumped them onto her bed where the open suitcase sat already half filled.

No, she hadn't been thinking of Kale in a business sense. Ironically, it was for that reason she'd been so quick, so certain, of her belief that he'd used his allure to deceive her best friend.

Was it so inconceivable that Tella was made of stronger stuff? After all, her interests at the time had involved elements that threatened her very safety. Whatever Martella may've been preoccupied by at the time, Davia was pretty sure Kale Asante's looks hadn't gone unnoticed by her best friend.

What woman wouldn't notice such a body and face? The athletic build, the length of him that had to top the six and a half feet mark at least. His skin was the tone of molten caramel. His deep-set stare possessed the same coloring. Not to mention his close-cut crop of light brown waves. The rich coloring was an attraction on its own.

Holding on to intense dislike in the presence of such an erotic distraction was virtually impossible and now it was only going to get harder. Now they were to be in close proximity for however long it'd take to unravel the mystery they'd inherited.

Davia had enough confidence in her abilities to know

she could set aside the allure of Kale Asante, but she still had to admit the man had far more going for him than his good looks. That quiet voice of his was deep but noticeably soft in its delivery. She wondered if he ever raised it. She mused it'd hold a raspy quality if he did. Such was the case with her own husky tone, she knew.

Beyond the voice, there were additional mannerisms that had captured her attention. The way he'd handled her elliptical, the slow brush of the back of his hand along the machine's bars and levers... She wondered if his touch was so gentle with other things.

Then there was the grin and the playful wince he gave when she'd managed to surprise him or challenge him on some point. She'd been attracted by his looks, but his mannerisms...those were the elements that had intrigued her.

And now you've got no reason to hate him.

Davia shook her head free of the unwanted reminder. No, if she took his explanation as fact, she had no reason to dislike him, but that didn't mean she could fall into bed with him. Well, she could...but should she? And why the hell was she even considering that? Aside from his comment about wanting to know if she was incredible to look at, he'd been the consummate gentleman. *She* was the one with her mind in her...lingerie drawer.

The accusation had her leaving the suitcase to check the aforementioned drawer for tights and other undergarments.

Davia was tossing an assortment of socks and underthings into the case when the doorbell rang.

She checked her wrist but found she hadn't yet put her watch back on. Then she looked to the small grandfather clock on the second-floor landing of her town home. She had over an hour before the car arrived. Davia gritted her teeth in dread of an unforeseen business emergency that might be about to throw a wrench into her plans.

She ran downstairs and was surprised when she opened the door.

"Kale?" She gave a self-conscious tug to the hem of the T-shirt she wore with an old pair of denim capris. Once again, she checked her wrist for the watch she still wasn't wearing.

"You're not late. I'm early." Kale met her gaze and smiled.

"I, uh, I thought you were sending a car for me?" Davia's tone was cautious, curious.

"I did." Kale turned from the doorway where his frame had eclipsed her view of the cobblestone drive beyond the courtyard where a silver Land Rover waited.

Davia blinked as if mildly stunned. "You drove?"

"I've been known to." His manner was playfully bland.

"So are you trying to make a statement?" Davia joined in on the tease.

"Trying to. I hope it's one that'll impress you."

It occurred to Davia that they were still in her doorway. Quickly she inched back to wave him inside.

"I've only got to get dressed and throw a few more things in my suitcase," she said.

"No rush. It's not like we're gonna miss our flight."

"Right." Inwardly, Davia gave herself a few mental kicks for behaving like a nervous girl on her first date. She was so *not* that and a date was so *not* what this was.

"I was just going to take a quick shower before I got dressed." Her tone was still breathy and anxious. She wanted to kick herself for real.

Kale laughed. "Davia, it's all right. We don't have bags to check. No security gates to clear. I'm ready when you are. Call down to me when you're done with your packing and I'll come up and get your suitcase."

"Oh, no, you…you don't have to do that," she told him, only to have him move into her personal space.

"I want to do that," he said.

Her actual height of five-eleven was greatly dwarfed by him. She admitted to feeling appreciatively overwhelmed and knew it was time to go.

"The kitchen's behind the bar around this side of the stairway…" she began in an airy, much lighter tone. As she motioned in the direction, she noted, "Just help yourself to anything you want." Then, turning, she quickly sprinted back up the way she'd come.

Only when Davia had disappeared around the corner at the top of the stairs did Kale look away. *Just help yourself to anything you want.* Her words reverberated in his head. He muttered an obscenity to criticize himself and wondered if he should tell her to be careful what she said to him.

No…he *shouldn't* tell her because it would confirm that solving the mystery of what she was like in bed had consumed the bulk of his thoughts since they'd met. Correction—since he'd seen that picture of her in Felton's file. And wouldn't *that* just take her right back to hating him?

Back to? Had the truth of what really happened between him and Martella Friedman changed or at least softened her perception of him? He wanted Davia to believe that hustling a woman into his bed was not the first thing he thought of when he conducted business. He wanted her to think that because it was actually true. He wanted her to think that even though all *he* could think of in that moment was having her amazing legs wrapped around his back and that smoky voice of hers moaning his name while he lost his mind inside her.

Muttering to himself, Kale charted a path for the bar and didn't stop until he tossed back a swig of her fine, locally brewed beer. Why the hell should he care about any of that? Before two days ago, he never thought he'd meet Davia Sands. Providing the truth about Martella hadn't even been a blip on his radar despite the fact that he didn't appreciate dark marks being put on his business reputation unless he put them there.

Now he was…what? Trying to pass himself off as a better man when he was nowhere near that? It was as he'd told Davia earlier. He had no interest in being that type of guy.

You did right by Martella. The quiet voice wedged in from his subconscious.

With a grunt, he took another swig of the beer.

Davia completed her packing and shower in record time. She left her bedroom carrying the weight of her suitcase, garment bag and tote with apparent ease. Impressive, when one considered the stiletto-heeled, mocha-suede boots climbed just above her knees.

Though he approved of the vision she was, Kale didn't hold much hope that the stairs, heels and luggage would play well together. He took the steps two at a time and relieved Davia of her things before she took the third step down.

"Nice boots," he said.

Davia glanced down. "Thanks. I thought so, too."

Kale hoisted the garment bag strap over a shoulder. "Not sure how well they'll go with an Iowa cornfield."

"I'm sure I won't be finding out." Davia's reply was full of humor. "My plan is to be in a pair of sneakers or hiking boots by the time I'm in range of one." She gave another look toward her stylish stems. "These are just for first impressions." *And to appease my unhealthy obsession,* she added silently.

Kale carried down the luggage with a fluid grace. "So we're trying to make a good impression? I should've kept my suit on, I guess."

"I think they'll take you seriously enough." Davia admired the quarter-length chamois suede jacket he wore with dark green hiking boots and a shirt of the same color that hung outside a pair of indigo jeans.

"So tell me why we're trying to make a good impression? I assume it's for more than the obvious reason of being polite."

Davia was making a quick check of her tote for anything she may have forgotten. "We don't know what we'll find when we get there," she said. "We may actually want to hold on to our inheritance. If so, we'll want our new neighbors to like us, right?"

"If so?" Kale set the bags down near the door and turned to face her. "Do you think you might sell it? I got the impression before that you wanted to keep it at all costs."

"Well, well, Mr. Asante, it seems *you're* the one who's thoughtfully listening now," she teased.

Kale shrugged, his smile indicating he might have been faintly embarrassed. "You're having a good influence on me, I guess."

Davia smiled approvingly and then sighed. "I've been thinking about our talk with Estelle Waverly. Ever since we hung up with her, I've been growing more suspicious of what we're stepping into."

Kale crossed to where Davia stood near an armchair in the expansive space that held a living room and a den on opposite sides.

"You're thinking she's not on the level?" Kale asked.

"It's not that." Davia quickly shook her head. "But I do get the sense that there's some kind of…drama involved and that it might play heavily into why my aunt and your uncle never got more involved with the property."

Kale moved past Davia to pace the living room. She noticed he was stroking his jaw and recalled that he'd done so in her office while they'd talked. The mannerism, teamed with the assessing look that took hold of his jarringly attractive face, made for a captivating mix.

"Do you remember what Estelle Waverly said when I asked if we were expected to attend that council meeting?" Kale said after a long, quiet moment.

Davia sighed again and nodded. "She said 'it depends on who you ask.'"

Davia admitted—and wasn't at all hesitant to do so—that there was a lot to be said for flying by private aircraft. The drive to and subsequent boarding of

Kale's jet had been leisurely and not at all marred by the frenzy and frustration generally associated with a commercial flight.

So much relaxation, however, played to the exhaustion that had mounted in preparation for the trip. Davia gave in to the need for a catnap some fifteen minutes after she and Kale settled in aboard the luxurious craft.

But while she had settled in, such was not the case for Kale. He'd been issuing silent commands to himself not to stare ever since he'd met her. He was determined not to play into any of the behaviors one might associate with the kind of man Davia had taken him for over the past several years.

After leaving her office he'd told himself it was, of course, her looks that had sparked his jaw-dropping reaction to her. Now he completely understood that that perception had merely been his way of avoiding the truth of it. Davia Sands's looks were simply one aspect of why he'd been so powerfully and unexpectedly captivated by her. Her poised, easy demeanor; the confidence in her words and outlook… Kale knew *those* elements had been the lure now reeling him in so effortlessly.

Davia had fallen asleep shortly after they'd boarded and Kale was grateful for the chance to ease up on his silent warnings against staring. With the woman at ease, he could stare until he'd had his fill.

A smile further defined the lush curve of Kale's mouth. Davia's breathing had deepened and he took a chance on satisfying a bit more of his curiosity. Slowly he allowed his fingertips to drift ever so gently along the line of her cheek. His smile deepened when he discovered her skin felt as silken as it appeared.

He was rubbing a few tendrils of her clipped hair between his fingers when Davia's lashes stirred to hint of her waking. Kale was cool in his retreat and had distanced himself by the time her eyes opened.

Davia woke with a small yawn and smaller frown as she worked to get her bearings. Finding Kale seated across the small aisle, she smiled.

"How long was I out?" she asked.

Kale raised a shoulder in a lazy shrug. "About forty-five minutes. We aren't even halfway there so you've got time to catch a few more z's if you want."

Davia gave in to another yawn. "I think I'm okay now."

"Get you a drink?" Kale offered, already pushing up from the swivel chair he'd occupied.

"Sure." Davia's face brightened with a cunning smile. "I need you to prove to me that you've got my beer on this plane."

"Sit tight." Kale was already bending to check the mini fridge behind the small bar in the rear of the cabin.

"It's good to know we've got a reach all the way back east," Davia noted.

"They were serving it at a party I went to out west," he explained while silently admitting he'd have visited the brewery had he known earlier she was part of it. "How'd you get into that business anyway?" he asked, retrieving two bottles of the chilled brew.

"What?" Davia feigned an affronted look. "Don't I look like a beer connoisseur?"

"No." Kale didn't blink when he gave the response unapologetically.

Davia took no offence and simply laughed. "It was

just a funny idea some friends from college kicked around one night. One night *long* after college." She laughed softer then. "We'd gotten together for drinks. The bartender gave us all funny looks when we passed on the wine. From there, the conversation took hold.

"We researched the idea. Then we actually thought we might be on to something and figured what the hell? Thanks." She accepted the bottle from Kale.

"Anyway, we all got very devoted to making it a reality. *That* while devoting time to our *real* jobs."

Kale's rich laughter filled the cabin. "Wonder what the bartender would think if he could see you guys now?"

"I think his bar was one of the first places to start carrying the beer." Davia raised her bottle to Kale in a mock toast before she took a swig. "I haven't thought about that night in so long," she said after they'd imbibed silently for a few moments. "The bartender didn't even try to hide his surprise. I mean, why would he? We were a group of Cali girls out for a night on the town, so obviously wine would be on the menu."

"Obviously." Kale chugged down another swallow of the brew.

Davia sighed. "I guess it's good to know I'm not the only one with the capacity to misjudge people."

"Can I ask you something?" Kale said after another few moments of silence had passed. "How'd you figure out or how'd you…come to the conclusion that me and Tella…that we'd slept together? Did she say something to give you the idea there was or could've been something like that going on?"

"No, not really." Davia straightened, pushing out of

her comfortable position on the loungechair. She appeared suddenly stressed. "It was nothing like that."

"So?" he prodded. "What was it?" He held the bottle poised while waiting on her answer.

Davia didn't seem in much of a hurry to provide one. "When she sold to someone in pretty much the same business that I was in, I just…figured it had to be about that. I mean…I could've matched your offer, Kale. Could've beaten it." She shrugged. "I just assumed you'd offered something I couldn't match."

Kale appeared thoroughly intrigued. He sat with his elbows to his knees. The bottle hung between his fingers and was almost totally forgotten. "But why would you think it had to be that and not that she was just too proud to sell to you?"

Davia helped herself to another swig of the frosty lager and realized he wasn't going to let the conversation end until she confessed all. She decided to just say it and be done with it. "Kale, have you ever looked at yourself?"

He straightened, total bewilderment taking hold of his features. "Looked at myself?"

Davia only watched him. Patiently, she waited for her words to click. She almost smiled when he blinked as awareness began to dawn on him. She looked on in complete appreciation of the adorable element the reaction brought to his gorgeous features.

"Oh," he said.

"Yeah." Davia nodded succinctly and then gave in to her need for a smile.

"Should I be flattered?" he queried in a slow, uncertain manner.

"You wouldn't be if you knew what I was thinking about you." Davia enjoyed a swallow of the full-bodied beer.

"Wow." Kale spoke the word reverently while stroking his smooth, strong jaw. "Guess I've now got some idea how women must feel when we men make assumptions based on their looks."

"Well," Davia sighed, watching the bottle while swirling the liquid inside, "if it makes you feel any better, it's my first time making that kind of assumption about a man."

"Any reason why I lucked out?" Once again, Kale seemed completely bewildered.

Davia couldn't hold back her laughter over his cluelessness. She raised her hand as if about to offer a testimony. "Somebody get this man a mirror," she groaned.

Chapter 5

Mullins, Iowa

It was approaching dusk when Kale and Davia arrived from California. A dark, roomy SUV sat idling outside the hangar where Kale's plane had been directed upon landing. Once the flight assistants had stored their luggage in the back of the vehicle, Kale and Davia were on their way to Mullins. The area was a wonderland blanketed beneath thick drifts of snow. The town was located about forty minutes outside the airport in Des Moines. Utilizing the built-in navigation system, they found the Waverly Bed-and-Breakfast with relative ease.

"Wow." The expression followed Davia's initial gasp when Kale pulled to a stop at the inn's wide, brick driveway.

Kale appeared equally impressed as he put the vehicle in park. "You think the rest of the town looks like this?" he asked.

Waverly Bed-and-Breakfast was the first stop when entering Mullins from the west. The place was a stately three-story building of stone, brick and glass. Golden light beamed from practically every wide window that adorned each level, giving the place the look of a gleaming oasis amid some dark, unfathomable expanse.

Kale and Davia just had time to trade prompt, approving glances before the red double doors on the front porch opened. A man and woman stepped out, waving to Kale and Davia. The woman moved further out onto the wraparound porch and urged the guests forward while the man headed toward their SUV.

"Here goes," Kale said as he left the truck.

Davia put a resolved smile in place as she exited the passenger side.

Kale and Davia's expressions were decidedly brighter by the time they shook hands with the ginger-haired Caucasian man who approached the SUV.

"Barrett Waverly." The man extended a hand and offered a generous smile that reached his pale green eyes.

Kale introduced himself as he accepted the handshake.

Davia did the same. "This is a beautiful place, Mr. Waverly."

"Thanks so much, Ms. Sands. We're proud of it."

Smiling, Davia shook her head. "Please, it's Davia."

Barrett Waverly's smile widened. "And you can call me Barry." He squeezed her hand between both of his and then glanced back toward the inn. "You should go on inside and get warmed up. My wife's ready to pamper you with your favorite drink." Releasing Davia's hand, he motioned to the SUV. "Help you with the bags, Mr. Asante?"

"It's Kale, please. And, yes, by all means." Kale took Barrett's hand in another hearty shake.

The men launched into friendly conversation while Davia carefully made her way toward the house. Though the brick drive appeared dry and well-treated, she still entertained the thought of black ice meeting the spiky heels of her boots.

The woman waiting on the porch had Davia's complexion and a petite, curvy build. She greeted Davia before offering her hand to shake. "I'm impressed," the woman said. "The last time I took that driveway in heels like that…it was the *last* time I took that driveway in heels like that!"

Davia laughed as she shook the woman's hand. "I thought this might be a good test of my stiletto-wearing ability," she said.

The woman threw her head back to laugh. "I believe it's safe to say you passed." She dropped her free hand over the one still clutched inside Davia's. "Estelle Waverly. You already met my husband, Barry."

"Yes. I was telling him how beautiful your place is." Davia cast another look up at the house.

"Let me show you around." Estelle kept hold of Davia's hand. "This is where Barry grew up," she explained as they entered the main hall. "When we moved back, we had the place completely remodeled and converted it to the inn."

"So you're not from here?" Davia asked when Estelle

released her hand. She watched the woman rush over to stoke the fire in the enormous hearth at the back of the great room they'd just entered.

"I'm not. Barry and I met and married in Seattle." Estelle stood in front of the hearth satisfied when the fire was once again burning high and bright.

"Husband and partner." Davia laced her words with a teasing air. "How do those labels get along in business?"

Estelle raised her hands, gesturing to the room surrounding them. "When 'business' consists of this, not bad at all."

The front door opened and with it came a frigid gust of air and the rumble of male voices and laughter.

Kale watched as Barrett set the baggage in paneled sections inside a wall just off from the main corridor they'd entered.

"This mini freight elevator will transport your things to the third level, where you'll be staying," Barry explained.

"Interesting system," Kale said.

Barrett finished loading the elevator and stood. "It provides the guests with more privacy. We use a system like this to transport everything from luggage to meals. Besides, there's no elevator, and neither I nor Estelle wanted to be carting bags all the way up to the third floor. Potential bellboys have taken one look at those stairs and run for the hills."

Laughter flooded between the two men as they continued their trek down the hall and into the great room.

After he was introduced to Estelle, Kale complimented her home. "I was telling Barry that this is quite a place you guys have here. It's a gorgeous thing to see when you're just arriving in a new town."

"Thanks, Kale, and there's plenty more to see," Estelle promised.

"But before we get into all that," Barry said, "let's get you guys out of your jackets and have you warm up near the fire."

"What's everybody having to drink?" Estelle called while Kale and Davia moved closer to the hearth. "We've got pretty much every kind of tea and coffee. Even hot chocolate or something stronger, if you like. Our bar is well stocked."

"I'll have whatever you do, Estelle," Davia called, taking great delight at the warmth gliding its way to her chilled skin.

"Tell me you've got brandy and I'm a customer for life." Kale rubbed his hands in brisk fashion in front of the flame.

Barry applauded. "Will a bottle aged twelve years do the trick?"

"It'll do more than that." Kale laughed and watched Barry head for the corner bar situated to the far right of the fireplace.

"How many rooms do you guys have here?" Davia asked Barry once the warmth had thoroughly penetrated her bones.

"Five to rent. Este and I have our own suite on this level."

Kale and Davia exchanged curious looks.

"You guys do well with such a small number of rooms?" Kale asked.

"You'd be surprised," Barry chuckled just as his wife returned to the room.

Estelle carried a tray laden with a plate of small sandwiches and a teakettle emitting a delightful fragrance.

"The fact that this is my hometown isn't the only reason we moved back and tried to make a go of this place." Barry shared the information as he handed Kale one of the two brandy snifters he'd brought over from the bar.

Estelle set the tray on a glossy, black-oak coffee table. The group sat in the four darkly cushioned square chairs surrounding it.

"There's lots of land in the area and that means lots of folks ready to build on it." Estelle passed Davia a mug of the fragrant Earl Grey.

"In the hope that there's a lot of money to be made," Barry added. "At any given time, contractors and their crews are in and around the area for some project or another. Given the amount of land and opportunity, that trend is set to continue for quite some time."

"With that kind of incentive, you'd think construction crews would be working 'round the clock," Kale mused after enjoying a slow sip of the brandy.

"Oh, they're here in major numbers, believe me!" Barry raised his snifter in a mock toast. "I work for a company that specializes in securing housing for contracting crews. About eight years ago the company decided to acquire its own property in the hope of cutting out the middle man—the hotel chains—and keep that cash in house."

"Just outside town, heading east, Barry's company has a larger hotel," Estelle said to Davia before taking a sip from the teacup.

"The inn is kept for the company heads who might see fit to visit the sites they're developing. My company's foray into housing was my idea and it proved to be a lucrative one." Barry gave a self-satisfied grin. "When I asked to oversee business in this region, they didn't argue."

Kale released a whistle into the big room. "That's some perk. Keeping a full-time job in Seattle and never leaving your hometown? Nice."

Barry sent his wife a meaningful look then. "We're hoping it could be nicer."

Estelle nodded and then turned to shift her gaze between the guests. "Barry has a spot on the town council. So far, they've been very successful in bringing many new businesses to the area, and that's sparked tremendous growth. Our proximity to a major metropolitan area makes us a desirable locale for people wanting the perks of suburban living without losing their connection to city life."

Barry's sigh amplified over the popping wood in the hearth. "There's another thing we'd like to bring into town. We'd hoped to save it for last, but there's been a lot of…discussion about it as of late and we don't think we can avoid moving it up on the agenda any longer."

"And this 'other thing' would be located on the property we've inherited?" Kale posed his question to Estelle. "Is that why you called us? Because there's been some resistance to whatever business you want to put there?"

Barrett sent his wife a baffled look. "Este?"

Estelle Waverly's dark, lovely face showed signs of strain and she set her teacup on the table. "I had a hunch that Kale and Davia might be a little…wary about making a trip out here. I remember all too well how I felt when you talked to me about coming here, and I didn't want them talking to anyone else and being put off about coming."

Barry reached out to squeeze Estelle's hand, the look on his face softening with understanding.

Estelle looked at Kale and then Davia. "I'm sorry, you two, about all the secrecy. Your being here is definitely important. You'll bring greater significance to what we're proposing."

"Which is?" Davia asked.

"What your aunt, Kale's uncle and Barry's uncle were trying to bring to this town."

"Something as American as apple pie," Barry chimed in. "A movie theater."

A few seconds ticked by as Kale and Davia stared at the couple, expecting them to say something more. Eventually, amused expressions crept onto their faces.

The Waverlys smiled, apparently not at all surprised by their guests' reactions.

Kale shifted in his chair, stroking his index finger along his brow as he moved. "No offence, guys, but giving a town a movie theater is not a bad thing. It can't be so bad that you need *us* to help sell the idea."

"It's not the idea itself, but what it signifies that, uh, poses the issue we're dealing with," Barry noted.

"Babe?" Estelle paused en route to picking up her cup. "Is it accurate to say we actually have an *issue* to deal with yet?"

Barry shrugged. "Well, I suppose we don't have one yet, but no one knows Kale and Davia are here or what their aunt and uncle may've told them about what went on here."

Davia moved forward in her chair. "What's my aunt and Kale's uncle got to do with all this?"

"The property you guys inherited—my uncle Chase Waverly was the original owner. I'm pretty certain that neither your aunt, nor your uncle, Kale, even knew they owned it. After my uncle died, my dad was privy to information about his business matters and he spoke of the less-than-diligent manner it seems his representatives used in trying to track down all the beneficiaries in his will. My dad was one, which is how I've come by the information I'm sharing with you now."

"Sounds like your uncle had some poor representatives," Kale said.

"You'd be correct." Barry's nod sent a shock of reddish blond hair sliding onto his brow. "But when one weighs in the fact that all this happened in the forties and that the beneficiaries in question were black, odds are high that he wouldn't have been represented much differently anywhere else."

Realization doused whatever humor shone on Kale and Davia's faces.

"This isn't about an inheritance, is it?" Davia asked.

Estelle finally retrieved her teacup from the table. "It's about a lot more than that," she said.

Kale shook his empty snifter in the air. "Think I'm gonna need another one of these, Barry."

Grinning, Barry clapped Kale's shoulder and left to see to the order.

"Estelle? What'd you mean when you said we'd bring greater 'significance' earlier?" Davia asked.

"Well, we understand that Bryant Leak and Gloria Sands had a love for theaters. One they passed on to their niece and nephew."

Davia shared a soft smile with Kale and then leaned over to squeeze his hand. She'd noticed his reaction to hearing his uncle's name.

"Those two had already gotten notice in their own local papers for being the first blacks to work for their town theaters," Estelle continued. "They gained some notoriety when their ideas for providing the moviegoer with a more...hospitable experience were taken seriously by their bosses."

"'A movie theater should feel less like a classroom and more like a living room,'" Barry said as he returned with fresh brandy for him and Kale.

"If that's a quote, it's a nice one," Kale remarked.

"I thought so. Your uncle said it." Barry grinned at Kale's stunned look.

"He said that and more. So did your aunt, Davia." Estelle curled up in her chair, tucking her legs beneath her. "We've got pretty much all the news clippings chronicling their accomplishments."

"Oh, I'd love to see those." Davia took the kettle from the low table and topped off her tea.

"We'll have them waiting for you guys tomorrow."

"You'll also get to see the property tomorrow," Barry added.

Estelle laughed. "If the rest of your shoes are like those boots, Davia, we'll have to make a stop by my boutique first."

"This is the last you'll see of them," Davia promised, "but I'd still love a trip to that boutique." She lifted her cup to toast the idea and then her smile lost some of its illumination. "Guys, I believe I can speak for Kale when I say we'd definitely support a theater being put on the property."

"Davia's right. We'll make it a place our uncles and Davia's aunt would be proud of," Kale said.

The Waverlys looked at one another. When Estelle gave a nod, Barry set aside his snifter. The weighted look had returned to his pale gaze.

"I suppose this is where we get to our...*issue*. You see, a theater is the last kind of establishment half the council, which represents half the town, wants here."

"Why?" Kale asked. "What could anybody have against the town having its own movie theater?"

"It's what the theater reminds them of," Estelle clarified, her bobbed hair swinging into her face when she shook her head.

"Which is?" Davia leaned in to the conversation.

Barry dragged a hand through his bright hair. "The theater is a reminder of how this town watched one of its own waste away from poverty and neglect because it was trying to prove a point."

"Wait a minute. All this because your uncle didn't mind letting two black kids give him tips on how to improve his business?" Davia sounded incredulous.

Barry shook his head. "No, Davia, all this because my uncle testified against the man who conspired to have those kids killed."

Chapter 6

"The evidence proved it all, but it was the press the trial got that saw Shepard Barns convicted of arson and attempted murder. 'Course he didn't get half as much time as he should have, but that's another story." Barry's expression was bland as he recounted the tale. "I don't suppose I need to go into details as to the motive?" he queried.

Kale grimaced. "We get the gist of it."

"My uncle Chase didn't even try to rebuild his house afterward. He put every bit of his energy into the theater, which Shepard half burned to the ground in addition to the house. The man was outraged by the idea of one, let alone two, black people trying to 'lay siege to Mullins,' was how he put it for the papers." Barry chuckled, but the gesture held no humor.

"I've got pictures of my dad before all this happened. Uncle Chase was his big brother. My dad said he used to go over almost every day after school to help work on the theater." Barry snorted a softer, equally humorless laugh then. "He said Uncle Chase actually thought he'd done something heroic by destroying that racist. Expected the theater to be visited by folks far and wide if he ever got it built. Aside from the kids, nobody came to help. Your aunt and uncle left shortly after the verdict came down. My uncle insisted. The local construction teams didn't even want to come back on the job even though it was the work they initially put into the place that Barns burned down. My dad said even his friends stopped coming by with their parents..."

Barry squeezed his eyes shut, smiling gratefully when Estelle moved close to clutch his hand.

"My dad said his folks even shunned my uncle and he wasn't far behind. Can you believe that? He was my dad's big brother and he did the right thing and they shunned him for it."

"Your uncle was treated like an outcast by an entire town because he testified against a murderer?" Davia noted as if disbelieving.

"The story's not so far-fetched," Kale said. "We're talking about the forties, after all. Such things are still happening today."

Davia knew it was true, though the reality was still difficult to hear. As if to ward off some inner chill, she clamped her hands around her warm teacup. "What you said about poverty and neglect, Barry...that was your uncle?"

Barry nodded. "By the end he was living out of one

room if you could call it that. My dad, being as young as he was, eventually changed his way of thinking. Said he loved his brother too much to see him that way. He did what he could to help, but it was hard seeing his brother like that. Plus, he was always getting in trouble with my grandparents and the rest of the family over turning their backs on their own kin. The summer my dad graduated high school, my grandparents pulled up stakes and hit the road. I think my dad was glad to leave. My uncle didn't want to come out of his hole. Still trying to make a point after all that time."

"It's a wonder nobody called the folks in the white coats," Kale dryly noted.

"No need," Barry retorted. "My dad said the man was saner than any of 'em. Didn't mind tellin' anyone who'd listen why he'd done it. Said he was holdin' on to the theater for the kids he was leaving it to. Maybe one day the world would be a place where creativity could thrive no matter where it originates."

Kale and Davia sat like stone fixtures in the chairs they'd occupied so casually moments earlier. They'd lost their taste for the beverages in hand, their minds racing with knowledge of events that had occurred before they were even born.

"I apologize for layin' all this on you both your first night in town," Barry said once he and Estelle had exchanged concerned looks.

"So no one ever had the chance to patronize your uncle's theater?" Davia asked.

"He died before he could finish it. Not that it would've mattered." A strange light appeared in Barry's pale eyes. "I doubt he even cared by then, if what my dad said is correct. My uncle was proud to be the theater's one, true patron. He loved it so much, he probably would've died there had the newly elected sheriff that year not sent his deputies out to drag him in out of the cold.

"The sheriff and my uncle went to school together and he was one of the few who didn't shun my uncle like the rest of the town. Uncle Chase had been living out there with no heat or running water... I suspect several in town didn't subscribe to the madness of the masses. No way could he have survived for as long as he did without somebody looking out for him. He held on to that property through it all, though. When the time came to settle the estate, my family didn't want to hear a word about the theater. My grandfather was in charge so my dad's hands were tied. Later... I think he just wanted to forget."

Silence settled thick and resolved but for the constant snap and crack of the logs amid the blaze that still thrived. Soon, Estelle was extending out from her curled position to stand and give a long stretch.

"My guess is we've all had enough for one night," she said.

"Este's right. Follow me. I'll show you to your rooms," Barry urged.

"You guys just yell if you need anything." Estelle began clearing away items from the low coffee table. "You're the only guests for a while, so you'll get the deluxe treatment."

"Thanks, Estelle," Kale said while following Barry to the stairway.

"We'll play breakfast by ear tomorrow. I'll have it all set out, so just help yourselves once you're up."

"Thanks, Estelle. Good night." Davia sent the woman a wave and then followed the men upstairs.

Kale let out a low whistle when Barry ushered them onto the inn's third floor. The trip up had taken a bit longer than customary with the new guests raving over the dazzling artwork and seating arrangements that hugged the walls and lined the corridors. Their arrival on the third floor simply brought forth more raving.

"Each floor has a guest lounge that offers a media nook, open bar and hot beverage caddy," Barry explained. "There're even gas fireplaces that can be operated by the guests themselves, but you'll find units in your rooms, too, if you prefer them to the central heating system."

Kale and Davia strolled the spacious lounge furnished with suede merlot sofas set atop thick, midnight-blue carpeting that ran the length of the rooms and corridors. Lending to the soothing allure of the plum-painted room was the glossy brick fireplace that Barry had spoken of. Its mantel was accented with framed pictures of the town of Mullins in days past.

"There's even a roof terrace if you feel brave enough to face our frigid temps and take a lofty view of your surroundings." Barry waved toward the ceiling where recessed lighting bathed the hallway in muted gold.

"On a night like this you could probably see the town lights from here," Barry explained. "It's nothing like what you're used to, but there's definitely a charm to it."

"I can believe that." Davia was already engaged by the fresh snow drifting past the windows where the drapes were drawn back.

"I should show you guys to your rooms before Este yells at me," Barry said, grinning.

Kale and Davia followed their host down the long corridor that was finished in the same rich plum color as the decadent lounge.

"The second floor has three guest rooms plus the lounge. This floor has two suites on either end of the corridor."

"Good to know." Kale was grinning more broadly. "Now I won't have to worry about Davia hearing me snore through the walls."

"That depends on how loud you snore," Davia teased back.

"Well, you won't be interrupted, so sleep and snore to your heart's content," Barry urged as they closed the distance to a looming door at the end of the hall. "The freight elevator I used to send up your bags earlier should have deposited them in your respective rooms."

"That's some trick," Davia marveled.

Barry shrugged. "Each room is equipped with one. It'll be shut down once you're inside your room—just a safety precaution."

"Got a high-tech place here, Barry."

"Glad you're pleased." Barry cast a grin across his shoulder to Kale. "We even serve breakfast by dumb-waiter, so just call down in the morning to request it if you'd rather eat up here."

They reached a tall, gleaming Blackwood door at one end of the hall.

"This is you, Davia." Barry unlocked the door.

"I hate to overuse the word *wow*, but wow," Davia sighed upon stepping inside the suite.

"No need to be jealous, Kale. Your spot is an exact replica," Barry said.

The walls, done in a rich almond tone matched another expanse of deep carpeting. A king-size bed was covered by a cashmere comforter of the same midnight blue as the carpeting. Crisp white linen peeked over the top, also casing the pillows and skirting beneath the comforter.

"Between the bed and the view, I may never leave this room." Davia had walked over to glance out of the window. "You can't always count on a spectacular view from the front and back no matter how pricey the place is."

In addition to the spectacular view, the room boasted a spacious bathroom. A desk area with a cozy eating space was positioned near the rear alcove where Davia stood marveling over the landscape.

"The winter views are incredible, given the snow and all, but you've seen nothing until you get a load of the view in summer with the sun rising or setting behind the cornfields. Incredible." Pride shone on Barry's face as he made the boast. He winced suddenly, though, and made a zipping gesture across his mouth. "I should really go before I start talking your heads off again. Kale? Can I show you to your room on my way?"

It was Kale's turn to wince. "Actually, Barry, I need to go over some things with Davia first."

"Sounds good. I'll see you both in the morning, then." Turning, Barry moved to a wall where he retrieved Davia's baggage from behind the panel that secured the mini freight elevator. He then used a similar key to lock the car and then handed both keys to Davia.

He handed Kale his room keys next and then saluted his guests.

"Good night to you both," he said.

When the door closed behind Barrett Waverly, Kale and Davia traded exasperated looks. Then Davia collapsed onto the bed and sighed.

"Bet you never thought such a small town would be in the middle of such high drama," Kale said.

Davia gave a throaty laugh. "If this were a TV movie, I wouldn't be surprised at all. But this…" She raised her hands toward the high ceiling and let them fall to the mattress with a decisive splat. "This I definitely didn't expect."

Kale walked the spacious room. "You still set on making a go of the property knowing there's…all this hanging around it?"

Davia sat up and began removing her boots. "Well, we still haven't seen it yet or heard what the council has to say." She gave a quick tilt of her head. "I'm willing to hold my answer till then." She grew rather solemn while tugging her feet free of the chic boots. "Chase Waverly was some kind of guy, huh?"

"Seems so, given what we've heard so far." Kale was nodding. "I got a feeling we haven't heard the half of it. Humph."

"What?" Davia asked of Kale's gesture and his resulting smile.

"Just thinking of some things my uncle used to say." He took a seat on the low windowsill. "They're starting to make more sense now."

"Like what?"

Kale rested his head back on the window. "He was

real big on doing the right thing. Always said being a man wasn't a designation based only on what you had below your waist, but in your heart and your head."

Davia's smile echoed approval. "Your uncle sounds like he had a good brain inside his head."

"Oh, he did." Kale's expression was a rueful one. "For a long time, I thought that the fact that my own dad didn't stick around lent to a lot of what he said. I figured he didn't want me to be that kind of guy." Kale pushed up from the sill. "Later, I started thinking that it wasn't my dad he meant, but some other man entirely—the kind who *was* the sort of man deserving of the designation."

"Chase Waverly sounds like he'd be deserving of the designation," Davia noted.

"He saved two lives, so I'd have to agree with you."

Davia watched Kale's easy expression grow tight, guarded. "Kale?"

He needed no prompting. "Saving a life was what I thought I'd been doing when I blindly involved myself in Martella's business. I guess, without knowing it, I was trying to live up to my uncle's perception of what a real man was." He laughed softly but the gesture carried a decided edge. "All I managed to do was put her back against a harder wall."

Davia shook her head to that thinking. "You gave her a way out and she didn't take it. Or…she did take it only to put herself into a deeper hole when she gambled it away."

"I should've found a better way." Kale massaged a drawn fist against his palm.

Davia left the bed, shaving off some of the distance between them. "What happened to Tella…what she did…Kale, it wasn't your fault. She needed the kind of help that went beyond money."

His grin betrayed none of the earlier edginess of his smile. While he rubbed the nape of his neck, he watched her with mounting interest. "I wish you'd stop trying to make me feel better."

"And I wish *you'd* stop making yourself out to be the bad guy." She gave him a tense, lopsided smile. "I think I've done enough of that and for long enough."

"Davia…" He drawled her name in a manner that urged her to stop.

She didn't listen. "If we're going to do…whatever needs to be done here, we're going to have to work together. That means no more harping on past drama. I'm sorry for the misunderstanding, Kale. I know you're not the kind of guy to use—"

His mouth was on hers before she could finish.

The act was seeking, hungry, claiming, and, at first, Davia could do nothing—nothing at all but stand there and take, welcome, enjoy.

Kale didn't seem to mind her inability to respond. The kiss heightened in intensity with his tongue making slow, lazy circles against hers and then repeating the action against the roof of her mouth. His hands fisted the lapels of her jacket and added more provocative stimuli to the act.

Davia could feel an urgency akin to possessiveness in the way he held her. The kiss began in the center of the room but the pressure of his mouth on hers, not to mention that of his body claiming her space and crowding her, sent Davia retreating as he advanced. Soon her back was meeting the wall. Hitting the barrier not only stopped her retreat, it stopped the kiss, as well.

Kale broke contact with her mouth but pressed his forehead to hers while he labored to steady his breathing. "Don't tell me I'm not that kind of guy. Seems I'll use whatever it takes when it comes to you. Good night, Davia."

He left her without another look back.

Frozen as she was, Davia could only stare after him.

Chapter 7

Kale half expected Davia to request her breakfast by dumbwaiter the next morning. He half expected—and he half hoped. The latter was for his benefit, though. He didn't want to see her again first thing in the morning. Not after last night. He made a fist out of frustration, taking advantage of the fact that his hand was under the table and out of Estelle and Barrett's view.

The couple had already been up for who knew how long when Kale arrived downstairs. He'd been led by his nose following the aroma of coffee, eggs, bacon and what smelled suspiciously of blueberry muffins.

He found Estelle and Barrett in the kitchen, and as he sat at the table, they discussed the plan for the day. First up was a visit to the property site later that morning.

"You'll probably lose your appetite for seeing it

after sitting through that town council meeting," Estelle called from where she removed a fresh batch of muffins from the oven.

Kale chuckled into his coffee mug. "That bad, huh?"

"It's been known to be." Barrett sighed, sitting down and helping himself to bacon before passing the platter to Kale.

"This all happened so long ago, it's surprising that it's still an issue." Kale accepted four of the hearty-looking strips.

Barry shrugged. "People tend to raise their kids with knowledge of the same drama they grew up with. Then they pass it on down."

Davia arrived in the kitchen then and Kale felt his hand, once again hidden beneath the table, draw into a fist. The last thing he'd wanted had been the very thing to happen. He'd told her the real story of his attempt to help her friend as opposed to taking advantage of her. Davia had seemed to take him at his word and then what did he go and do? He proved he was exactly the kind of guy she thought he was from the start. *Nice goin', K.*

"Morning, everybody." Davia sent the blanket greeting and was greeted by the group. "Estelle, that coffee smells as good as the tea did last night," she commented while moving into the kitchen.

"Thanks, girl. It's a local blend from a company out of Des Moines." Estelle laughed when she glimpsed Davia's surprised look over her shoulder.

"That was my reaction, too," Estelle went on, "but once I tasted it, I had no complaints or doubts."

"It smells fantastic." Davia continued to rave and went to pour herself a cup at the sideboard.

"Davia's into local brewing herself," Kale informed the Waverlys while Davia worked on her coffee. "Got her own beer label and everything."

At the sideboard, Davia smiled broadly as the couple voiced their surprise and interest over the news. "My partners and I have a few Midwest restaurants carrying the brew, but you'll probably have to head out to Des Moines to find them."

"You might want to talk to Rich and Troy Ayers while you're here," Barry said while breaking open a blueberry muffin. "They own the local sports bar."

"Oh, that's a great idea. I discovered that Des Moines coffee brewery after a few cups of the stuff at Rich and Troy's place," Estelle said.

"Those guys detest anything imported," Barry explained. "They'd probably be open to finding another good domestic beer to add to the menu."

"That sounds like a plan. We could head over to Ayers for lunch after the council meeting," Estelle suggested.

Barry slathered butter to one side of his muffin. "You should call over there first and have a table waiting. The place is likely to get stampeded after the meeting."

"You make that council meeting sound like quite the event, Barry," Kale said.

"It is!" Barry practically bellowed. "More so today given what's up for discussion and having you guys in attendance."

"We were just telling Kale that we want to take you guys to the site before the meeting." Estelle went to get fresh plates and silverware for Davia who had just settled at the table.

"When do we need to be ready?" Davia reached for one of the huge muffins.

"Oh, there's plenty of time, so eat up." Estelle took the liberty of filling Davia's plate with some of the fluffy scrambled eggs and several slices of the thick bacon. "You're gonna need this fuel when that wind hits you out there." Estelle set down the loaded plate. "You guys must've turned right in when Barry took you up."

Kale and Davia made a point of not looking at each other then.

Davia cleared her throat and smiled. "It seemed so late."

Estelle laughed. "Probably because we spent so much time talking. Plus, the days are shorter and you guys had already packed so much into your day with traveling and all. Probably made it seem much later than it was."

Barry was standing, his plate and coffee in hand. "Well, we won't talk your heads off just yet. Enjoy your breakfast. We've got some things to do around the inn." He looked to Estelle who was taking her plate to the sink. "We'll head out to the site in a few hours. Give you guys time to head back here and change for the meeting. Sound good?"

"We're in."

Davia was thankful for Kale's confirmation. She was uncertain about being alone with him and was finding it rather difficult to speak.

The Waverlys left the kitchen and, for a while, only the sound of utensils against plates filled the silence. Davia rose to top off her coffee even though she didn't need to.

"I know what happened last night probably has you

thinking you were right about me all along, but if you're expecting me to apologize for it, I won't." Kale's rich voice seemed to echo across the kitchen. "I've been wanting to kiss you since I met you. It's pretty much all I've been thinking about. You probably hear that line from men so much that it's pathetic and, for that, I'll apologize. I just can't think of a better way to phrase it."

Davia remained turned to the sideboard. "Well, now you've eased your curiosity." Her voice carried a phony, refreshed tone. In the time it took her to blink, she felt him at her back. He didn't touch her, not even when he set his hands on either side of her against the sideboard.

"You really believe that?" he asked.

"What should I believe?" she countered, turning to him.

His molten-chocolate eyes wandered her face in an almost hopefully bewildered fashion. "You should believe that I like to spend my time doing what I think about."

He kissed her then and Davia could think of nothing other than responding. She would've settled back against the edge of the sideboard, but there was no chance to.

Kale had moved his hands from where he'd set them in the makeshift trap along the sideboard. He skimmed the backs of his hands, powerful and elegant, along her sides, outlining the curve of her figure. Then he was using those hands to cup her bottom and pull her snug against him.

Davia's hands weren't still, either. She indulged in the moment to mold them to the sculpted plane of his chest beneath the black fisherman's sweater he wore. A slave to the desires of her hands, she was curving them over his broad shoulders and up to his nape. Lightly, she grazed the fine hair tapered at his neck.

Soft, distinctive sounds of sheer hunger left Kale's throat. They kept an easy rhythm to the thrusts his tongue made against hers—thrusts that deepened each time Davia gasped and allowed him more room to explore her mouth.

His grip firmed on her bottom and then he was tugging Davia closer until her feet left the floor. Instinctively, she locked her legs around his waist, her fingers curving tighter into his hair to draw him closer and deepen their kiss.

Kale suckled her tongue deep into his mouth, keeping it locked there in a manner that both relaxed and stimulated. He released it only to recapture it seconds later and begin the act all over again. He found her reaction to him to be an undoubted enticement, but somehow Kale managed to break the kiss. He appeased his hunger for her then by targeting the curve of her jaw. The elegant line of her neck, he treated to a succession of openmouthed kisses until he was applying his lips to her clavicle.

He made an honest effort to speak, but could—at first—only groan his pleasure. Finally he triumphed over his desire. "Davi?" he murmured.

Davia warmed at her name shortened and sounding sensually tormented on his tongue.

"You're gonna have to stop me this time." His voice was still a tormented murmur. He set her to her feet, but still feasted on her clavicle with the irresistible openmouthed kisses.

Hands free of her derriere, Kale eased his curiosity about what her breasts would feel like against his palms. Deliberately, he took their fullness in his hands, wrapping his fingers over the long-sleeved mauve tee she sported with a pair of black yoga pants.

"Davia, please." He was treating her nipples to a delicious thumb massage. "Stop me," he begged.

"Why would I do that?" Her teeth grazed his earlobe. She was potently aroused and pleased to be in such a state.

"Davia." Kale's voice was muffled as his face was buried in the side of her neck. He inhaled desperately, somehow finding the will to exercise the cooler head. He eased back, raising his hands to keep distance between them that time. He looked away, frowning fiercely and blinking as though he were making an attempt to recover his bearings. This wasn't the time and it definitely was not the place, he told himself.

"You should eat," he said upon focusing on the table and latching onto the first excuse he could find for leaving her alone. "It's gonna be a helluva day," he added.

Davia, still clinging to the sideboard, waited until Kale was gone before she sighed. "You can say that again."

About three hours later Kale and Davia stood in the midst of the property they had inherited from Bryant Leak and Gloria Sands by way of Chase Waverly. To most anyone else, the area would instill more despair than inspiration.

Kale and Davia, however, were undeniably inspired. The Waverlys had driven their guests to the tract of land about ten miles outside the Mullins town limits. Desolation would perhaps be another accurate descriptor. The label was one the entrepreneurs could agree with as they observed what lay before their eyes.

The fifty-acre tract of land was an expanse of wintry-white dotted intermittently with tufts of snowcapped brush. In the center of the space stood the brick construction that held Kale and Davia in a captive state.

"It's a theater. I—" Davia gave a mystified shake of her head. "I knew that was the project, but I didn't realize…so much of it had gotten under way. I didn't think your uncle had accomplished nearly so much."

Chase Waverly's confidence in his project was evident if one took the stately signage standing some fifty yards beyond the construction as fact. Overgrown with weeds and nests that were home to a variety of species, the decades-old marquee still carried its fading message. The message was painted in large block letters against burned-out lights, many of which were missing. The billboard atop the tall, brick post read C M G TH S UMM R.

"Coming this summer," Kale said. "They really were working on it." He looked to the building in the distance. It was equally overgrown with weeds and vines, and coated with snow.

"Yes and no," Barry told them. "Mr. Leak and Ms. Sands had been more involved at the planning stage. That required lots of interaction with community leaders for the requisite permits and such." He looked around the abandoned lot. "My uncle saw no cause for concern and everything was going smoothly. His plans to build the theater had been highly supported. The bank was quick to loan him money, sure they'd make a quick turnaround on the deal."

"Until they saw they'd have to deal with two black kids to get the job done," Kale finished, not even trying to mask the biting tone in his voice.

Barry nodded, his own expression a grim one. "Chase couldn't risk that, so he asked them to let him take the reins on that part of the business. Without that loan, my uncle may've been sleeping on the street."

The comment earned Barrett Waverly a couple of curious stares from his guests.

"This is where Chase Waverly lived out his days after the trial," Estelle explained. "He funded the first part of the construction from his own pockets. The banks were interested in the project until after the trial. Then they wouldn't loan him a dime. He lost the house in the fire Shephard Barns started, used the insurance money to put as much into finishing the theater as he could."

Kale and Davia looked back at the unfinished construction with new interest.

"This is a disgrace," Davia said.

Barry nodded. "That's true in all kinds of ways, going all the way back to my dad and his friends helping out around here. The day they put the chairs in the upper level, my uncle had a family day for the kids to come and pick their favorite seat. After the trial, folks wouldn't even let their kids ride their bikes down this way."

"Those kids are grown now, grandparents probably," Davia snorted. "They should be ashamed of keeping this going."

"Sins of the father," Estelle sighed.

Davia rolled her eyes. "More like stupidity of the father."

"Why didn't the bank ever foreclose?" Kale asked. "The theater never opened, they never made their money back."

"That was the sheriff's doing. Sheriff Jesse Fitzman to the rescue," Barry said as he waved a hand in the frigid air. "His brother was bank president at the time. After all Uncle Chase had been through, the sheriff talked his brother out of taking everything from him. The Fitzmans had money to burn even then. The amount my uncle borrowed wasn't much even in those days.

"Before the theater, he'd owned the town pharmacy. He'd mortgaged it for the theater, so that went to the bank and they say Sheriff Fitzman paid the difference out of his own pocket."

"Well, the sheriff sounds like a good friend to have," Kale said. Then he turned serious. "Barry, you know we're within our rights to build whatever we want on that property. So what exactly is the plan here? Aside from the necessary building permits and such, none of us have to be concerned with pleading to these people's sense of decency or lack thereof."

Barry reached for his wife and pulled her close. "This isn't about the property, Kale. It's about getting folks to come together and support the place, its... potential. In doing so they would acknowledge the wrong that was done and maybe the town can get on with the healing it's done without for way too long." On that note, the Waverlys strolled off arm in arm.

Kale bent to pick up a handful of snow as Davia scanned the property, silently envisioning its potential.

"You think a movie theater can cure racism?" Kale asked.

Davia smirked, looking away from the horizon. "They've tried everything else. Why not this?"

Kale watched the snow cascade from his palm. "Is this what you want, Uncle Bry?" he wondered aloud.

Davia leaned down to squeeze his shoulder and he caught her hand in his free one.

"I don't know if this is the best thing or the craziest thing I've ever done, Davia, but I want in."

Again, Davia turned her hazel eyes toward the property. Then she gave Kale's shoulder another squeeze. "So do I. So do I."

Chapter 8

The town of Mullins unarguably epitomized the phrase "small town quaint." During a January winter, that phrase adopted a more defined meaning. The day was an overcast one with the threat of another snow-filled event looming over the town.

Barely into the third week of January and Christmas lights still held their place of annual importance with the wreaths adorned in their dominant spots. Multicolored lights hugged the lampposts that lined the streets and doors of the local shops.

It was like a painting, Davia thought as she took in the view from the backseat of the SUV Barrett Waverly drove down Main Street. Davia could easily imagine Norman Rockwell coming there to be inspired for one of his well-known portraits depicting the wholesome lifestyle. Mullins was the kind of place folks most often referred to when they wanted to relay the beauty of small town living.

They'd headed for town following a return trip to the inn where they'd changed clothes after the visit to the property site. They'd left in plenty of time to guarantee an early arrival for the meeting and to grab their seats before the other attendees arrived.

Barrett Waverly had gone to take his place behind the long, cherry-wood console reserved for the council members. Estelle had gone to speak with the receptionist they'd seen on the way in.

Town hall, the venue for the meeting, held the same all-American charm as the rest of the town. Davia looked away from Barry preparing his notes, to Kale, who stood making a call on the other side of the room. From time to time, he looked at his phone as though he were scanning a document before he started to speak again.

For just a few moments Davia squeezed her eyes shut. Once more, she processed all that had occurred during the last few days. There was no hope of ranking it all in order of greatest to least importance. Everything had come together like some perfect patchwork quilt. Every piece was a vibrant and necessary part.

The inheritance and the story behind it, Kale's revelation about Martella and now... Davia looked at Kale again. His behavior at the land site had intrigued her. Though her perceptions of him were already shifting, it wasn't until she watched him there at the site that she'd really captured the truest glimpse of who he was at the core.

This was about more than the promise of financial gain for him. She could see that. Not that there was ever any *real* promise for that—not the sort that he was used to his project generating. Even so, she knew a movie theater in a small Iowa town wasn't exactly his usual type of endeavor.

Watching him out there, sinking his finely gloved hands into the snow as he remembered his uncle…it was more captivating for her than any of the considerable charm he unconsciously or consciously oozed.

Then there was the kiss—*kisses*—they'd shared. But right now was definitely not the time to dwell on them.

Kale was finishing up his call and returning to claim his spot next to Davia when Estelle arrived along with a pretty, auburn-haired woman and a man who was almost as tall as Kale.

"Kale Asante, Davia Sands, I'd like you to meet Mitchell Barns and Cindy Fitzman, two members of the town council." Estelle made the introduction.

"It's Mitch to my friends and associates," the well-dressed blond man said following handshakes. "I visited that swanky theater you did in Des Moines, Kale. Quite a project."

Good naturedly, Kale dipped his head and smiled. "I hope you enjoyed it."

Mitch Barns, grandson of the infamous Shepard Barns, threw back his head and let out a hearty bellow. "Oh, yeah, me and the wife had a fine time for sure!"

"Looks like we've got the right people on hand if we want to bring the movies to Mullins," Cindy Fitzman said. She was a small woman with a perfectly round face framed by a wealth of auburn ringlets.

"We've heard a lot about your grandfather, Ms. Fitzman," Davia said. "He sounded like he was quite a man."

"That's right!" Mitch chimed in before Cindy Fitzman could respond to the compliment. "Sheriff Fitz was a hero to so many people around here."

"But a real pain in the ass to your family and their friends, right, Mitch?"

The practiced ease fueling Mitchell Barns's grin waned a tad and he turned to Barrett, who had spoken from his place behind the seating console. "We all want what's best for the town, Barry, you know that."

"But best for *who* in town—in your opinion?" Barry tossed back.

"Oh, look," Cindy interrupted before Mitchell could rebut their colleague's challenge. "There's Fred and Moira Wiley. Estelle, we should introduce them to Kale and Davia."

With that, the budding, tense conversation was effectively silenced.

Twenty minutes later all parties were in place and the meeting was being called to order. The hall was packed. Word had spread quickly of Kale and Davia's presence and several more interested residents were on hand.

"Is it just me or did the place not resemble a ghost town outside?" Davia leaned over to ask Kale while the meeting was being called to order.

"You're right. Where did all these people come from?" He gave her a sideways look. "Chances are they'll want us to say something. You up for that?"

"Are you asking *me* to do it?" Davia whispered.

Kale gave a little shrug. "I don't have a problem with you speaking for me," he whispered back.

"That's sweet of you, but I don't know how much patience or tact I'd have for addressing the likes of Mitch Barns and his circle." She acquiesced with a lopsided smile. "Although we *do* want them to spend time in our establishment."

Kale grinned. "Guess that means I'm nominated."

"You're such a gentleman."

Kale caught the inside joke. "I already told you I'm not. I've damn well shown you, too. Now hush up. Sounds like we're getting started."

Davia stifled her reaction and rebuttal to Kale's words and focused on the situation at hand. Mitchell Barns had the floor and had already made use of it.

"...*And* judging from my brief conversation earlier with our polite and accommodating new visitors, our distinguished Councilman Waverly has already wooed them over to his side!"

Conversation among the council as well as the audience grew in volume and intensity.

"It's all true, folks!" Mitch Barns continued to state his case over the mixture of raised voices. "Councilman Waverly already has Mr. Asante and Ms. Sands tucked away all nice and cozy at his inn!"

The room's volume rose to an almost deafening pitch then.

"Order! Order!"

The sound of a gavel banging its plate pierced the melee and Estelle looked over to give Kale and Davia a concerned look.

"I was afraid of this," Estelle said.

"Order!" Council chair Lucille Clancy had scooted to the edge of her seat while pounding the wide cherry-wood gavel. She settled back a bit once order had resumed.

"I'm sure we all appreciate the situation at hand," the chairwoman began. "I'd like to thank everyone here today for their patience. It's understandable that many of us are passionate about this issue, but I'm sure we can all agree that now is not the time for accusations." The stately gray-haired woman cleared her throat and presented a refreshing smile to the crowd.

"Perhaps it'd be a nice change of pace to hear from our guests, Kale Asante and Davia Sands, the owners of the property the town is eager to see transformed." The chairwoman raised her hand in a beckoning manner. "Mr. Asante, Ms. Sands? Could we impose upon you for a few words?"

Kale sent Davia a sly, knowing look and then stood with seamless ease while buttoning the salt-and-pepper jacket of the tailored three-piece adorning his enviable physique.

"Thank you, Madam Chair—Lucille." Kale graced the woman with a killer smile when remembering to address her by first name as she'd insisted when Estelle Waverly had made the introductions.

Davia noticed the woman's bashful smile and knew that Kale's charm had just scored him several points. Briefly, she bowed her head to hide her smile.

"I'd like to thank the town for such a warm welcome today," Kale began. "Many of you stopped by to introduce yourselves and shake hands. Neither myself nor Ms. Sands—" he turned to look down at Davia "—have knowledge of all that your town has endured in the shadow of what happened so many years ago. We can only focus on what inheriting this property means for us. We were each very close to the people who left us the property they inherited from Barrett Waverly's uncle Chase and we want to honor their original plans for it. Our intention is to finish the theater."

Kale made a point of consistently shifting his stance so that the sound of his voice was equally spread across the expanse of the crowd. "It was important to them. My uncle and Davia's aunt made theaters important to us, as well. Such projects are ones we've based our careers on. That's really our stake in this—not to change perceptions of past events or even your way of life other than to add the convenience of your very own hometown venue to enjoy one of the most fulfilling and easiest means of escape I've ever known."

Kale paused when the crowd murmured at his insight. "Ms. Sands and I fell in love with your town at first sight and we'd love to be part of its continued flourishing." He gave an intentional pause then. "With that," he continued, "it'd be wise for you to think of others who might feel the same. New residents from the construction teams already here to the ones who'll possibly be arriving as my and Ms. Sands's hoped-for project gets under way.

"These people will have families. Some will be looking for a place to settle. What do you want them to see, to feel, when they get here?" He looked at Lucille Clancy again. "Madam Chair, thanks for letting me have the floor." Kale looked at the audience next. "Thank you all, as well. Now, if you guys will excuse us, we want to enjoy more of your town." He sent a single nod to Davia who stood and offered a polite smile to the crowd. Taking Kale's hand, she let him lead her from the silent room.

"I'm gonna guess you got an A on persuasion in speech class."

Kale pretended to ponder Davia's statement as they walked. "Hmm…it was often a challenge getting to that class, but I was able to…persuade my professor."

The couple shared a laugh while strolling arm in arm along the quiet street. Despite the high attendance at the council meeting, there were still signs of life inside the shops along Main Street. Through frost-crusted windows, Kale and Davia could see people going about their business, smiling and chatting despite the drama stewing inside their town.

"You think they care?" Davia asked, peering inside a barbershop window they passed.

"Probably aren't even aware of this little crisis," Kale said, looking inside the shop window, as well. "Especially the transplants. New residents often have no connection or interest in the town's history or its past trouble."

While Davia considered that, Kale moved close to brush his fingers along her hairline.

"Snow seems to love you," he said when she blinked in surprise at his unexpected touch.

It was then that Davia noticed the heavy gray clouds were delivering on their promise of snow. She sighed. "I know this stuff can be a headache for those who have to live in it, but for someone who rarely sees it, it's like a dream—a good one."

Kale wasn't fixed on the snow. His gaze was focused solely on Davia. Her mention of a dream did stick with him and he was in total agreement that it—*she*—was a good one.

A quick, tapping sound filtered through the snowflakes. Kale pulled his eyes away from Davia to the man behind the window they stood in front of.

Kale gave Davia a nudge and she, too, turned to acknowledge the smiling man who then moved from the window to open one of the tall redwood doors of the establishment.

"Afternoon, folks," the man greeted. "You two gonna catch your deaths standin' still out there like that. You guys need some help?"

"We were at the town meeting," Kale said as he hiked a thumb over his shoulder in the general direction of the hall. "Thought we'd get some fresh air," he finished.

The man's smile became a grin. "That doesn't surprise me. Most of our newcomers get sick of those meetings after a few visits. Not sure how lucky we are that there's still enough natives to fill all the council seats."

The man gave a sudden shake of his head as though realizing he'd gone off on a tangent. "Least you can do is come in and warm up."

Kale and Davia accepted the offer with eager nods. They stepped past the glossy wood doors into a warm sports bar and were instantly glad that they had. The scent of spices and apples awakened their nostrils as soothing warmth melted the chill that had taken hold of their skin.

The man stood closest to Davia's height. He had a broad build and smiling green eyes that seemed to twinkle as he spoke.

"I'm Rich Ayers. I run this place with my brother Troy. You probably met him during the meeting," he said. "He's one of the council members. Reluctantly."

Kale's gaze narrowed. "Why reluctantly?"

Rich's grin renewed itself. "All due respect, sir, but you saw what a circus that was. Would *you* want to be part of it?"

"I see your point." Faint laughter accompanied Kale's words.

"We may not have a choice but to attend more than our fair share," Davia was saying. "Especially if we decided to build here."

Rich Ayers tugged a hand through the tousle of brownish-blond strands covering his head. "You two the ones who inherited Mr. Waverly's land?"

"That's right. Mr. Waverly left the property to my aunt and Kale's uncle." Davia introduced them and gave a brief rundown of their plans and how the idea had gone over with certain members of the town council. "Not sure Mr. Barns is up for it," she tacked on.

Rich chuckled while leading them into the quiet establishment. It was cozy, despite its sports bar allure. There were peaceful nooks for eating and cushiony soft areas for enjoying preferred spirits.

The quiet drone of the TV tuned to a twenty-four-hour sports channel mingled with the easy stream of a country-and-western melody. The music wafted through the speakers posted high in the building's rafters.

"Would've been worth it to see old Mitch get riled

up," Rich mused. "Half the time he walks around actin' like he knows something the rest of us don't. No…" He shook his head. "I'm happier holdin' down the fort right here."

"Well, it's quite a place." Davia scanned the environment with an appreciative eye. "We're staying at the Waverly inn and Estelle Waverly said she had the best coffee here. Loved it so, she now has it stocked at the inn."

"True, true." Rich nodded enthusiastically. "We take pride in providing our patrons with a variety of items to whet their whistles."

"Even locally brewed beer?"

Rich Ayers eyed Davia then with a mix of interest and male appreciation. "Beer connoisseur, huh?"

"I'm a partner in a local brewery out of California," Davia shared.

"No kidding?" Ayers sighed. "I was already impressed. Now you've just got me stunned."

Kale had remained quiet, enjoying the log-cabin style of the interior design. Gradually, he tuned in to the little repartee between Davia and Rich Ayers. Kale fixed on the bar owner and the way the man's eyes roamed Davia. While the need to break the guy's jaw didn't immediately spike through him, Kale decided he'd probably have to hate the man on principle.

Whatever the case, it all took a backseat when Davia took Kale's hand to lead him along to a cozy spot Rich Ayers had picked out for them to wait on Barry and Estelle. It was no chore at all for Kale to forget everything but her warm hand against his.

Chapter 9

"That sounds like a product we'd definitely want here," Troy Ayers said sometime later as he stroked his whiskered jaw. "I'm ashamed to say we don't already have it. We pride ourselves on keeping a lookout for quality craft brews."

"Don't beat yourself up about it," Davia said. "It took me and my partners a lot of time to convince our earliest clients that folks from Cali could make more than wine."

There was laughter and then Rich Ayers was instructing one of the servers to fix up the group with another round of whatever drinks they'd been enjoying.

"I think I want a new flavor of coffee," Estelle directed.

"Ha! Gotta give our best customer what she wants," Troy told the server. "And we should talk about arranging a tasting with your partners," he said to Davia while Estelle gave her new coffee request.

"We can make that happen." Davia raised her coffee mug in an obliging fashion and smiled.

"We got a habit of carrying all our Des Moines beers on tap," Rich was telling Davia. "We'd most likely do the same for you, especially if there's a chance we could get you to put down stakes in our neck of the woods."

"Ah, that's a shame, Rich. I'm a Cali girl born and raised."

Davia's words drew laughter from everyone except Kale. He merely smiled.

"You may surprise yourself, Davia," Estelle taunted. "I never thought I'd be anything but a Seattle girl, but being out here…it's been quite a life."

"You're sure there's nothing that could ever make you give up that fast pace?" Rich teased as he probed.

Davia laughed. "You'd be surprised how many opportunities I've had to slow things down out there. I guess I'd consider it if there was something that was worth it—something I just had to have, couldn't live without."

Troy laughed. "Well, let's hope it's our soon-to-be movie theater."

Glasses and mugs were lifted in toast. Everyone took a moment to enjoy their respective beverages.

"You guys think everyone might eventually get on the same page with this?" Davia queried. "Kale gave a great speech at the meeting, but I've got the feeling that Mitch Barns and his friends might take a little more convincing if he's as against it as he seems."

"They'll take more than *a little* convincing, darlin'," Rich predicted.

Rich, Kale and Davia had chatted a little over twenty minutes before the front doorbell chimed to announce the arrival of new customers. The council meeting had adjourned shortly after Kale and Davia's departures. Rich had contacted his brother by mobile and asked him to tell the Waverlys where they could find their guests. A while later the group was sitting down to their first round of drinks.

"Mitch has got no good reason to be so against the theater other than the fact that his grandfather was *so* against it," Rich was saying.

"You guys think we'll have any issues once building gets under way—if it gets under way?" Kale asked the brothers.

The question grabbed Barrett Waverly's attention. He was fixed on Rich and Troy's pending responses as he accepted a fresh brandy from the server.

"I'm sure Mitch wouldn't risk the attention," Troy said. "Causing that kind of trouble would bring him a lot of it."

"Hell—" Kale grimaced "—is the guy *that* obsessed with upholding his grandfather's philosophy?"

"If he's not, he puts on a good show." Barry fiddled with the stem of his snifter. "It's a damn shame, too. Mitch's dad used to help my uncle after school, just like my own dad did. Before they all turned their backs on him over bigotry. It's gotta end."

Rich raised his beer bottle. "Amen," he said.

Everyone else mirrored him in word and action.

* * *

"Our apologies for the day going downhill, guys," Barry was saying as he and Estelle walked into the inn with Kale and Davia.

"Would it be okay with everyone if we push back dinner a couple of hours since we had that big meal at Ayers?" Estelle suggested while she hung coats in the front closet.

"Sounds good to me," Kale called. "We can play it by ear. I doubt I'll be in the mood for another big meal today."

"Agreed." Barry and Davia spoke at once.

"Then it's settled," Estelle said. "If no one has any objections, I'm gonna turn in early."

"Another good idea," Davia championed.

The Waverlys headed off to their bedroom suite. Kale offered his arm to Davia and together they ascended the stairway.

Reaching their floor, the two silently, albeit mutually, agreed to stop by the guest lounge. Both dropped to the first sofa they approached and rested back against it.

"Still want in?" Davia slyly queried.

"Yep." Kale chuckled lazily. "Am I an idiot or what?"

Eyes closed, Davia smiled. "Guess we both are since I still want in, too." She grunted laughter then and pushed up on the sofa. Leaning forward, she studied the red accordion folder lying on the coffee table.

"Looks like Estelle left us those news clippings," she said as she thumbed through some pages.

Kale, still relaxing back on the sofa, opened an eye to a narrow slit. "Lot of work for a small-town paper in the forties."

"Maybe it'll give us some ideas for the project."

"True," Kale said, but he made no move to sit up and take a closer look at the big file. "I'll have to put it off till later, though. I don't think my eyes are capable of focusing. Estelle had the right idea about turning in early."

"Agreed." Davia sighed. Forgetting the folder, she leaned back against the sofa. "Now all we have to do is make it to bed."

"Mmm...good luck with that. I'm good right here."

Drowsiness renewed, Davia shut her eyes. "So much for the gentleman carrying the lady to her bed."

Kale's lazy chuckle returned. "Trust me, if I carried you to bed, there'd be nothing gentlemanly about it."

Davia chuckled then, too, but the need for deep sleep had all but consumed her. Soon, both she and Kale had tumbled into a deep slumber, oblivious to the fresh snow that fell against the windows emitting the waning beams of sunlight.

Davia woke feeling a little off-kilter despite being well rested. Languidly, she assessed her surroundings. Slowly, she raised her head toward the windows to find that night had fallen.

She was tucked inside the crisp, warm sheets of her bed, with no memory of how she'd gotten there. Her thoughts went to Kale, but sadly he was nowhere to be found.

Davia turned onto her back and repeated the words in her head. *Sadly, he was nowhere to be found...* Did she want him there next to her? She believed that went without saying, but was that for the obvious and shallow reasons or was there more motivating them?

Deciding she was still too groggy to ponder such ideas, Davia threw back the covers and got out of bed. Aside from the jacket and hiking boots she'd worn that day, she was otherwise dressed. Whew!

Smiling over the fact, she went to pull more comfortable attire from a drawer. After a quick shower, she dressed in a flannel sleep set consisting of a waist shirt and shorts. Barefoot, she left her suite. She spared a quick look inside the guest lounge on her way past. She only half expected to find Kale there. With a deep, slow exhale, she steeled herself to continue toward the only other door on the hall.

"Knock twice and then go," she told herself.

What exactly was the plan once she got to his room? With any luck he'd be asleep. Otherwise, she'd launch a conversation on their true purpose for being there.

Davia was at the door and knocking when she realized she should've grabbed the folder from the guest lounge. There was no time to make a run for it. Not long after she knocked, the door was opening and her jaw was dropping.

Kale had answered decked in only a pair of PJ bottoms that hung dangerously low on his lean hips. Irresistibly sleep-sexy, he rested his head against the side of the door and gave her a drowsy smile.

"I, uh, I'm sorry." She saw that he'd been just as conked out as she was.

Kale's molten-brown stare took a slow, undeniably meaningful scan of her body. One corner of his mouth tilted up and he eventually brought his eyes back to her face. "There's no reason for you to apologize," he assured her and stepped back from the door. "Wanna come in?"

"I can't." She wanted to, though. Oh, how she wanted to. "I, um, I only came to thank you."

"And of course staying in the hall is the only way you can do that properly?"

Ignoring the suggestion in his words, she smiled. "I didn't mean to wake you. I just wanted to thank you for putting me to bed. I guess I must've dozed off on the sofa."

"We both did." He leaned on the door again. "Guess the day was longer than we realized."

Davia nodded. "Well, I'll let you get back to sleep."

"Are you serious?" Though he didn't explain his comment, she saw it in his eyes. He was awake now. And feasting on the sight of her. He rose to his full height and gave her a curious smile before opening the door wider. "Come in, Davia."

Again, her hazel gaze fell to his chest. Creamy brown, sleek and broad, it called out to her and she could almost feel her fingertips tingle from their desire to crawl across it.

"Kale, I can't." She closed her eyes as if to fight an inner war with herself.

Once more, he resumed his leaning stance on the door. "You want to, though."

Davia leaned in, too, taking up residence on the door-jamb.

"Don't worry, Davia. I get it."

"Do you?"

He shrugged. "This has all got to be confusing as

hell. All the mess we've got between us. Tella and now this project on your aunt's and my uncle's behalf."

"It's not about Tella, Kale," she argued, looking down at the deep carpet peeking between her bare toes. "I believed what you said about what happened, but you're right. Now we've got this new business between us and—"

"And it goes without saying that business and pleasure are the last things we should be mixing."

She raised a shoulder to acknowledge the truth. "You know it can get messy."

"It can, but sometimes it can be worth it."

"But *often* it can be messy. Too messy."

Kale reached out to toy with the hem of her sleep shirt. "Sometimes the mess is what makes it worthwhile."

"Sometimes," Davia agreed warily.

Kale gave her shirt another tug. "You obviously know where I sleep. I don't believe in locked doors."

"You lead a very risky life," she teased.

Kale grinned, offering a languid half shrug. "The risk can make it all worth it, too." His expression was sober. Even though his words held a lightness, his demeanor gave off an opposing emotion.

"It wouldn't be wise for us to start this, Kale."

"Why?"

Smiling, she nodded as though unsurprised by his comeback. "It wouldn't be wise for me. Besides this project, our lives are very different and…very distant. Even though the promise of a few days of supreme sex is beyond tempting—" it was why she'd come knocking on his door, after all "—I try to go into these things hoping for something more."

Kale suddenly crowded her against the doorjamb. "And you think I can't feel the same?"

She met his stormy gaze full-on. "I believe you're capable of it, but it has nothing to do with us and why we're together here."

He closed what remained of the distance between them. "What things become is rarely what they start off as and the outcome is not always so obvious."

"And if it doesn't become anything, how's that going to affect what we're trying to do here?"

"I've got no clue." He dipped his head to skim his nose across her jaw. "But right now do you really care?"

Chapter 10

Davia's thoughts blurred. She couldn't think straight, not when she was pummeled by the powerful sensation of Kale's mouth devouring hers and the stirring in her stomach as his fingers disappeared beneath the hem of her shirt and into the waistband of her sleep shorts.

She took advantage of easing her curiosity about what his bare chest would feel like against her fingertips. She walked them across the taut plane, until she was linking her arms around his neck and playing in the smattering of baby-fine curls along his nape.

Kale's fingers weren't still, either. Once he found her nude beneath the shorts, his fingers slid inside her, parting her, giving him room to arouse her clit. She found it as pleasurable as he did, no doubt. Her mouth went slack as she emitted a moan around his tongue. Dragging his mouth from hers, Kale traded hard, hot kisses to her lips for soft, wet ones along her jaw and neckline.

Davia began to ease her body up and down along his fingers as they claimed her two at a time. They stood against the jamb, wound in a sultry lock. Davia's second thoughts had long since fled. Her thoughts now were fixed on a single ideal—pleasure. She found Kale's mouth again and launched another kiss, taking his tongue with the same neediness as she accepted his touch at the part of her that ached for all of his attention.

Kale timed the thrust of his tongue to that of his fingers. They lunged and rotated inside the deep, warm well of Davia's sex. He ended the kiss when he felt her inner muscles seize and allowed himself the pleasure of watching her beautiful face as she climaxed. When it was over, he felt aftershocks continue to claim her body.

Kale refused to relent, even when she turned a pleading gaze his way. Thumb still stroking its treasure, he leaned close to nuzzle her ear with his nose. "Would you like to come in now?" he asked.

His lips were smooth as they skimmed the elegant line of her clavicle. They were just inside the door with Davia's back flush against it. She smiled, inhaling the fresh scent of soap that clung to his skin and hair still damp from a shower, she assumed.

"You didn't sleep long," she noted, her tone drugged, mellowed. She threaded her fingers through his curls while making the observation.

"I got enough, don't worry." His voice carried on a guttural chord.

There was soft laughter on Davia's part that curbed

on a gasp when Kale began a slow suckle of her earlobe. His fingers found their way beneath the hem of her shorts and set about reclaiming her.

Davia went to her toes and then draped a leg over his hip in a desperate attempt to offer as much depth to the caress as possible. Kale was turning to her for another kiss, his hand smothering her nape as he held her close to accept it.

His free hand went to work on her sleep shirt, the buttons of which he freed with skill. Davia gave a weak shimmy of her shoulders and the garment fell away. It was swiftly followed by the shorts that matched it.

A single lamp emitted soft glowing light across the otherwise darkened room. The illumination drew attention to their bodies and the effect for Davia was overwhelming. "Kale," she whispered.

"Please don't ask me to stop," he countered.

Davia's laughter was enveloped in a gasp when Kale used the tip of his tongue to outline the shell of her ear before he rotated it inside the canal.

"My legs are about to stop working," she warned him, and found herself hoisted against his chest shortly after.

Kissing resumed with ravenous intensity. Davia could feel herself floating, but she didn't dare open her eyes to investigate. Instead, she gave more of herself to the kiss, emitting quiet, provocative sighs with every tilt and arch of her head.

Kale didn't break the kiss. He simply scooped up Davia and carried her into his bedroom. His palms were cupped firmly around her derriere, his fingers positioned so that they just grazed her feminine folds.

Davia shuddered when the tip of one of those fingers took possession. She couldn't resist offering herself for a deeper claiming. She had no idea how long it took to reach the bed. She was far too wrapped up in the sensations from his lips and fingertips. Still, she celebrated the feel of soothing linens on her skin when Kale put her on her back and followed her down. He spent a few more enjoyable moments with her mouth before making his way along the soft curve of her jaw.

Kale lingered at the base of Davia's throat, driving his tongue into the hollow he found there. He cradled the sides of her breasts, the move giving him leave to stimulate her nipples beneath his thumbs.

The quiet room filled with the sounds of Davia's approving sighs. Kale made his way lower, skimming the rise of her bosom while intermittently dipping into the deep valley between.

Davia's back curved into a perfect bow and she was needy for the touch of his lips closing over the peaks of her breasts. Kale had other delights on his mind, though. Bypassing Davia's pert, heaving chest, he slowly kissed his way down to her navel.

Kale tongued the silken, circular dip until Davia squirmed uncontrollably. Setting his forearm to her belly, he quelled her movements and then took possession of her upper thighs. Once they were firmly in his grasp, Kale simply dragged his nose across the waxed triangle of flesh above her sex, inhaling her scent before he went further.

Davia jerked in place when his tongue found its target. As it lapped and suckled at her clit, his hands tightened on her thighs, holding her still for more. She moaned a guttural sound of arousal. She could feel him using his tongue to tease apart the folds of her sex before driving inside. Immediately she was lost in blissful wonder and eagerly arched her hips, squeezing his tongue as it thrust and rotated.

Kale took her vigorously in that manner for several minutes, but stopped short of allowing her to careen into orgasm. While she lay there panting upon the tangled bed sheets and working up curses to scold him for stopping, Kale reached inside a brown leather valise that sat open on the night table. Withdrawing a condom, he used his teeth to tear into the packaging while dragging the PJ bottoms off his hips.

Seamlessly, he put the protection in place and claimed her in the next moment.

Davia's gasp melded with Kale's groan as the sensation of taking her all but consumed him. Clutching one of her thighs, he raised the toned limb high near his waist to deepen his penetration and their enjoyment.

Davia bit down on her lip and surrendered herself to his possession. Taking fistfuls of the bed linens, she sighed Kale's name repeatedly and with mounting rigor. Her hips undulated in a sensuously slow rhythm that brought deeper moans welling up from her throat.

Her moans were practically drowned by the savory groans Kale uttered with every rich stroke. Rising, he braced on his knees and kept his grip on her thighs, tugging and drawing her hips closer as if he couldn't possess enough of her.

Davia wanted to wrap her legs around his back and squeeze to her content, but Kale wouldn't allow it. He kept her thighs spread, almost flat to the bed.

His warm gaze sparkled more vibrantly as he followed the casual glide of her fingers across her flawless dark skin. His shaft tightened in the telling fashion that signified he was on the threshold of climax.

Kale's restraint splintered when he saw Davia outline her navel with her thumbnail before gliding her hands upward to cup her breasts. His need flooded the condom and the sounds of his climax echoed in the room.

Davia followed Kale into bliss seconds later. Together they readily tumbled into a mindless abyss of elation.

"What?"

"Hmm?" Davia tried and failed to lift her head. She was too mellowed out by the aftermath of what she'd just experienced to motivate herself into doing more.

Kale gave her head a nudge where it rested on his shoulder. "Why'd you say my name?" he asked.

"Mmm...does there have to be a reason? I've been saying your name all night."

"Sounded like you wanted to ask me something just now."

"And I've been asking you things all night, too." She smiled, feeling his soft chuckle vibrate through his chest and into her cheek.

"Is that what you want to ask me now?"

Soaking up another few moments of the enjoyment she found in his embrace, Davia pushed herself up to sit. "I was about to take us back to an earlier conversation." She propped on her elbows and fixed him with a sidelong look. "What you said about selling only to me and why you'd do that. You could've made a lot more money posing your offer elsewhere and then you wouldn't have had to deal with someone who had such a low opinion of you."

"Call it me never being able to resist a challenge," Kale replied, slurring his words, still feeling deliciously sated.

Davia sat up then, disregarding her nude state. "I'm not such a challenge anymore, though, am I?"

He raised an eyebrow. "You really think that? If anything, you're even more of one."

"And how do you figure that?"

Kale pushed up slightly then, too. Rolling over, he covered her beneath him. "You're in my system now."

She wound herself around him, arms looped at his neck while her long legs curved around his waist. "Guess we'll just have to stay here until I'm out of it."

Kale dropped lazy kisses across Davia's neck and shoulders. "I'm afraid it's not that easy."

"Yeah." She positioned her mouth into a mock pout. "We do have business to handle, don't we? But…" She locked her ankles behind his back. "Seeing as how we *are* Barry and Estelle's favorite customers, it'd surely be no trouble holding on to our rooms for a little longer."

Kale nibbled at her earlobe. "I like the sound of that. But how's it supposed to get you out of my system?"

Some of Davia's playfulness eased and she regarded her lover more warily. Who said she wanted to get out of his system?

Before she could retort, Kale spoke again. "You asked me a question," he recalled, settling back as he studied her face intently. "Why sell to you of all people?"

Davia silently ordered herself not to get lost in his chocolate gaze. "Well?" she prompted.

"Would it surprise you to know that I hadn't made that decision until I got to your office? Selling to you was the obvious choice once I met you."

"Would I have had to sleep with you to get you to make good on the deal?"

"Not at all, but I couldn't have gotten what I wanted without making that deal."

She used her hip to nudge him a bit. "But you've already gotten what you wanted."

"Not quite, Davi. What I want is to stay connected. This property keeps us that way."

Davia's wariness increased. She studied him at length, not sure if she wanted to give thought to what it was she suspected.

"You don't really know me, Kale," she said at last.

"A very good reason to stay connected, right?"

Davia opened her mouth, not sure if she was about to acknowledge or dispute his reasoning. She had no chance to do either. Kale was kissing her again.

Chapter 11

Davia woke to two surprises that morning. There was a superb-looking breakfast that had been delivered by dumbwaiter and sat ready to be devoured in the bedroom alcove. The bedroom itself was the next surprise. She was still in Kale's. Not that it was such a surprise given the weakest streams of morning light had been peering through the drapes when she'd drifted into sleep following a fourth round of lovemaking.

She saw that he wasn't there in the room with her and was about to call out to him when he returned.

"How'd you sleep?" he asked after watching her from the doorway for a moment.

"Briefly," was her response along with a sly smile.

"Sorry about that." His style of reply clearly stated

that he was anything but. He shifted a look toward the alcove. "Hungry?"

"Very." Davia sent an interested look to the alcove, as well. "Will I have to leave bed to get it?"

Kale eased his hands into the pockets of his PJ bottoms. "You leaving the bed is half the fun for me, but only if I get to watch you do it wearing nothing at all."

"I see. And what's the other half of the fun?"

He came to the bed at a slow approach and caged her beneath him. "The other half is to sit across from you and watch you eat wearing nothing at all."

Carefree laughter vibrated from her throat. "Eating in the buff never much appealed to me. Is there something else you'll settle for besides that?"

Kale helped himself to a sweet, slow peck from her lips and then eased back to search her eyes with his. "Tell me you'll come to Miami with me when we're done here."

"Kale…" Davia's easy demeanor betrayed her then. She shook her head once. "Are you joking?"

"Do you think I am?"

She searched his extraordinary stare. "No, I… I don't think you are and I don't get why."

"Why what?" His voice carried the edginess of challenge. "Why I'd want you to eat in the nude or why I'd want you to come back with me?" He spoke the last while trailing his mouth down her neck.

"Yeah, that." She could barely speak the words. "That last one."

He suckled the sensitive spot below her ear. "Does that mean you'll do it?"

"We've both got work to get back to, remember?

Don't you think it'd be too hard to get the kind of bed time we'd both want once we left?"

"Bed time?" He moved away from suckling her skin. "Is it too far-fetched to believe I could want more than that?"

"Kale? Relax, okay?" A measure of relief had returned to her light eyes. "There's nothing more you need to prove to me, all right?"

"Is that what you thought I was doing?" His mood was gradually darkening.

"I just don't want you to think you have to pretend there's anything more than sex on your mind for us," she went on, clearly having no idea as to the downward turn of his mood. "I wouldn't hold it against you," she added.

Davia gave a languid stretch beneath him. "This was very much needed and appreciated. It'll definitely be an incentive not to miss any business meetings we might need to have in the future." She followed the tease with a hard kiss to his mouth and then released a playfully tormented groan.

"That breakfast smells too good." She wiggled out from his loosened hold and left the bed to eat in the buff just as Kale had wanted.

Sadly, he was in no frame of mind to enjoy the sight. Resting back on the bed, he dug the heels of his hands into his eyes and brooded.

"Hey, you're up," Davia called when Kale arrived in the guest lounge that afternoon. "Barry and Estelle went out to handle some business for the inn. They told me we could help ourselves for lunch," she explained.

"Have you eaten?" Kale walked into the lounge, dressed in a T-shirt and sweats. A pair of socks was all that adorned his feet.

"Yeah, I ate a little something while going through these clippings." She motioned to the items set out on the coffee table. "I made you a sandwich, too." She gestured to the bar console where a fresh pot of fragrant coffee awaited along with the food.

Kale took a half and then grabbed a beer from the mini-fridge beneath the bar. "Anything good in there?" He took a bite of the sandwich and motioned toward the clippings.

"Oh, gosh, yes," Davia raved, shaking her head in wonder over all she surveyed. "It must've taken Barry and Estelle close to forever to put all this together. It's a lot of really useful and fantastic stuff." Selecting one of the items, she waved it in Kale's direction. "Many of these would make great accent pieces for an entryway to the lobby of a theater."

Davia went on, but Kale's responses became quieter and gradually drifted into nothing at all. The silence eventually got Davia's attention.

"Everything all right?" She watched him at the console, dusting his hands free of sandwich crumbs. "Are, um, are *we* okay?"

Kale turned but maintained his silence as he looked at her.

"You were pretty quiet before I left your room earlier," she noted.

He leaned against the console. "You're the thoughtful listener. Did I sound like there was anything wrong?"

"Kale, we—" She turned her eyes back to the clippings and photos without really seeing them. "We just met. We just...slept together..."

"And I just told you I want more than that."

"I told you I didn't need or expect that, Kale."

"Well, maybe I do."

"Which is a problem for a number of reasons." Davia sighed.

"Right..." Kale lost his taste for the beer. He put it down and massaged his neck. "Right...there's distance and we don't know each other and you don't trust me."

"Kale, please." She shook her head. "I told you this wasn't about Tella."

His gaze narrowing, he watched her curiously. "I can see that you believe that. I don't get why *I* can't."

"I'm sorry about that," she said, though she didn't sound eager to make up for the fact.

Nodding as though resolved to accept her response, Kale took the plate with the other half of the massive roast beef and chicken sandwich Davia had prepared for him. He helped himself to the juice that also sat on the console. Balancing the glass on the plate, he stopped by the coffee table and gathered up a few of the clippings folders.

"You done with these?"

Davia only nodded and Kale headed out of the lounge. Alone, she pressed her fingertips to her eyes and groaned.

"What the hell is your problem, Davia?" she asked herself.

* * *

"I'm going to have a platter made for Kale. He'll hate himself for missing out on one of Luella's steak and shrimp specials."

Davia smiled across the table at Estelle. "I'd be careful divulging so many town secrets to outsiders. Especially when they're secrets *this* good." She forked up another decadently tender scallop and closed her eyes while savoring the taste. She dined with the Waverlys at Luella's Steakhouse that evening. Kale had bowed out for the night.

Davia had remarked on the place being a perfect date-night spot upon arrival. The atmosphere was just right with its candlelit chandeliers and bronzed centerpieces. Hunter-green tablecloths complemented the wine-colored carpeting and seat cushions. Immersed in the serenity of the environment, Davia fixated on her plate of scallop linguine with greater approval.

"You and Kale should stop here for dinner before you leave town," Estelle was saying as she dipped a morsel of shrimp into a spicy red sauce.

"Well, at least I can go on and mark a visit off *my* list. So can Kale when he gets the takeout you ordered."

Estelle turned her gaze toward the ceiling. "I *hope* he gets it. Barrett's in the back taking care of it, but he and Luella's husband Ed are big college basketball fans. Doesn't matter what time of year it is, they can talk for hours about a previous or upcoming season if they have the chance."

Laughter followed the insight, but it wasn't long before Estelle's expression harbored something serious. "Actually, I meant this would be a great spot for you and

Kale to enjoy…as a couple, before you leave town." Estelle gave a guilty shrug when Davia's head snapped up.

"Sorry, girl, you'll have to forgive me. I'm a romantic at heart." Estelle fidgeted with a tendril of her bobbed hair and looked around the softly lit dining room. "If Barry were out here, right about now he'd be telling me to cool it with the matchmaking, but it's obvious the two of you are interested in one another."

Davia sent the woman a sly knowing look. "Because he's incredibly gorgeous, right?"

Estelle rolled her eyes again. "Well, that's obvious, but I'm sensing it goes deeper than that."

"Geez." Davia regarded her scallop ruefully. "We must be pitifully transparent. We've only been here for a couple of days."

Estelle shrugged. "Speaks of how intense things are between you, I guess. *Beyond* what's happening with the theater."

Davia sat a little straighter, as if the woman's words had astounded her.

"I'm sorry, Davia." Honesty gleamed in Estelle's dark eyes. "Guess that's another thing my husband's pegged right about me—I'm unfailingly nosy."

"No." Davia shook her head as she laughed. "Me and Kale…well, we've got drama between us that no one could help but notice…and for good reason. I misjudged him about something." She voiced the confession after a lengthy silence. "We just cleared it up a few hours before we got here. I was at fault and I apologized for it. But, Kale… I don't think he believes I'm done with it."

"Are you?" Estelle asked.

"I think so." Davia squeezed her eyes shut quickly.

"I mean, I have to be if we're going to work together, right?"

"Was it about business?"

"Not exactly."

"Hmm." Estelle looked as though she had enough information. "So you and Kale had the personal going before the business kicked in."

Davia breathed out a laugh. "This might all be easier if 'the personal' was the fun kind."

"This would seem like the perfect time and place to change that, you know?"

Davia reciprocated Estelle's coy smile. "You've got a naughty mind, Mrs. Waverly."

Estelle laughed outright. "A naughty mind makes for a happy marriage."

"Please!" Davia laughed then, too. "I seriously doubt we'll be courting our way into marriage. You know, Barry's right about you. You're definitely a romantic."

Barrett Waverly's voice was next to ring out over the table. "I was wondering how long it'd take for her to start matchmaking."

Davia looked up, prepared to join in with Barrett's resulting laughter. Her breath caught when she saw that he hadn't arrived at the table alone, but with Kale.

"Look who I found!" Barrett raved.

"Hey, Kale." Estelle beamed. "We were just talking about you."

Barry squeezed his wife's shoulder. "We got that, Este."

"Hush, Barry."

"So what's with the folder, Kale?" Davia was desperate to move the conversation along. Her breath caught when he simply stared at her for an extended moment. Then he smiled a rakish smile and followed the gesture up with an even more rakish one before taking his seat at the cozy round table.

"You were onto something earlier," Kale told her. "Using the photos to decorate a theater lobby," he clarified when she gave him a befuddled expression.

"Oh, that's a terrific idea!" Estelle clasped her hands and settled back against her chair.

"I thought so, too." Kale's smile dimmed after a moment. "Unfortunately, all our planning won't mean much if we don't have the support of the council, isn't that right, B?" He'd taken to calling his host by his initial.

"Yeah...they could definitely put the kibosh on the whole thing." Barry's earlier glee now showed signs of failing.

"But it's our land, right?" Davia noted.

"It's still zoned commercial, Davia," Barrett said. "That means we'd still need the blessings of a few town officials before we could move forward with any projects."

"Which means permits," Kale shared.

"But you've got a way around it?" Davia's tone was hopeful. She smiled obligingly when Kale gestured toward her wineglass, taking a sip when she nodded.

Looking to Barry and Estelle, Kale slid two photos across the table. He'd taken them from the folder he'd arrived with. "What do you see?" he asked the couple.

The Waverlys studied their respective photos for a while.

"Well, this looks like Lucille Clancy—a younger version." Estelle referred to the town council chairwoman. She showed the photo to her husband.

Barry observed the snapshot for a moment and then shook his head. "No...that's her mom, Rosetta McClure."

Estelle whistled. "Wow, I never would've guessed such a proper lady owned a pair of roller skates, let alone used them." She marveled. "I bet Lucille would get a kick out of seeing this."

"Not sure her mom would." Barry chuckled and looked over at Kale with a curious smile. "What's your plan?"

Chapter 12

Davia turned from the tall, guest lounge windows when she heard Kale walk into the room.

"How was your dinner?" she asked. They had just returned with the Waverlys from the steakhouse an hour earlier, with Kale's dinner.

Kale closed his eyes as though he were savoring the memory of the food. "I don't know if it'd be a better idea to move here for dinner at Luella's every night or to just hire her husband as my personal chef."

Talk of relocation, no matter how playful, took Davia's thoughts back to their post lovemaking conversation that morning. Davia rested back against the windows and ignored the chill penetrating the glass.

"That was a good idea tonight, very commendable."

Kale shrugged, recalling what he'd suggested while

they were all still at the restaurant. "It's only commendable if it works."

"Why wouldn't it work? People love old pictures and reminiscing about back in the day."

"I just wonder if it'll be enough."

"Time will tell."

Kale's expression soured over the remark. "If we only had more of that, right?"

"Kale—"

"Save it."

"We shouldn't be fighting."

"We shouldn't?" Kale put on a look of phony confusion. "What should we be doing? I know…" he added before Davia could summon a response. "We should be picking up where we left off before dawn."

Intrigue shone in her eyes. "I didn't think you were interested in that."

Kale moved deeper into the lounge. "That'd be true if we were picking up from where we left off just after dawn, but since you're not interested in that—"

"Kale—" Davia interrupted again, but had even less time to continue than she had before.

Kale didn't interrupt her with more words, though. Instead he was backing her securely against the windows and taking her mouth beneath his.

Davia was happy to let herself forget whatever she'd wanted to say and take part in his plan that was more suited to her desires then anyway.

Kale used his thumbs to make slow circles along her jaw and then he stroked the back of his hands across her high cheekbones.

Davia's soft, pleading moans heated the desire already burning his veins.

Her slate-blue jumper was a warm and alluring fit to her svelte frame. Secure as the fit was, however, it couldn't match Kale's determination. With an expert touch he easily undid the intricate row of snaps winding down along the zipper.

Next, Kale started on the buttons lining the cashmere sweater she wore beneath the jumper. He might've freed her of her clothing faster had he spent more time with the fastenings and less time nipping and gnawing his way along her neck.

Davia, almost completely absorbed in Kale's touch, could still hear his voice near her ear.

"Is this all you want from me?"

Davia decided she wouldn't risk him stopping by giving him an answer. Her legs went weak when he suckled her earlobe while continuing to remove her sweater.

Needy for the feel of his skin on hers, Davia turned her focus to the denim shirt that he wore beneath the sweater he'd already shed. She undid the first three buttons and then shrieked when the crisp cold permeating the lounge windows met her bare back.

The top of the jumper hung at her waist. Kale's sole focus was in undoing her bra, the final barrier between him and what he wanted.

Davia rolled her head across the glass, arching into Kale while he cupped and nuzzled her breasts in pursuit of freeing them. Her fingers mingled with the velvet curls at the back of his neck and she arched her body with greater insistence. She was hungry to feel his mouth on her breasts. Kale didn't disappoint, but saw to one nipple with his lips and tongue while tending the other with his fingers.

Davia's hands trembled as she attempted to finish undoing his shirt. She was unsuccessful, especially when Kale traded the petal-soft kisses to the tip of her nipple for a suckling that skirted this side of harsh. Davia winced as pain and pleasure overtook her on a strangely balanced wave. She bit her lip, only mildly stunned that she was on the verge of climax from the sensation. He was too good at this.

Then, suddenly, he was gone. It took Davia a second or two to process his departure; she was still basking in mounting orgasmic waves. Lashes fluttering, she forced her eyes open and took a moment to collect herself and regret the solitude.

Slowly she tugged the sweater and dress just over her elbows and turned back to enjoy the snowy view of the night. Craving the cool on her heated skin, she rolled her forehead on the frosted windowpane, sighed and prayed for the chill to reduce the fever Kale had fanned inside her.

Such was not to be and Davia decided to turn in for the night. Hopefully, sleep would prove effective in reducing her intimate fever as well as her lurking confusion.

She was tugging her clothes into place when she felt herself being jerked out of them again. Kale had returned. Davia was still facing the window, but she could feel his bare skin against hers. He'd removed his shirt during his absence.

Soon her jumper and tights were pooling the low heels of her gray riding boots. He hadn't removed his pants and she could feel his belt buckle boring into the small of her back when he leaned in closer. Her bra was next to fall and Davia gasped as the cold glass met her hot breasts. The shock didn't last for long; Kale cupped one mound in his palm. His free hand skimmed her torso, until his fingers were toying with the lacy stitching along the waistband of her panties.

Davia let her head fall back to his shoulder, her fingers raking at the glass pane in a desperate, seeking manner. She so wanted to touch him, but it was clear he wasn't in the mood for tenderness.

His breathing held a labored sound, as though he were being tortured. He pressed kisses behind her ear and along her nape, tasting her with quick, probing laps from his tongue. Her heart rattled beneath her rib cage with its jarring beat and sent the blood roaring against her eardrums. She heard the clink of his belt buckle as he undid it, then the rasp of his zipper.

With the fingers of his free hand he skimmed her only remaining scrap of clothing for just a few seconds more. Then they dipped inside the silky material and smoothed across the feather-soft mound of curls above her sex.

One brush, then another, and then those fingers were staking their claim. Middle and ring finger speared high into her heat and moisture. Davia cried out her pleasure into the glass. Her eyes were almost closed, but she could still glimpse the sight of her own breath fogging the cold window. She sobbed his name in tortured response to the sensuously slow assault at her core. His thrusting fingers roused tremulous moans from her throat as she quivered between his hard, heated body and the hard, frosty glass.

Kale took a condom from a side pocket of his jeans. He'd left Davia earlier to go and collect a few. The jeans eased down his powerful thighs and calves as he held on to a quivering, aroused Davia. He tore into the packaging while purposely slowing the thrusting rotations of his fingers inside her body.

Arrogance curved his mouth with a smile while he relished the sound of his name uttered from her X-rated mouth. His erection was almost painful to touch, he was so starved to have it surrounded by her. He endured, slipping the protective sheeting in place with an impressive finesse given the circumstances.

His arrogant smile mingled with something akin to possession. How had that happened? he wondered. Her existence wasn't even a blip on his radar before a few days ago and now... Now her existence was practically everything to him.

He nipped and sucked at her earlobe while he claimed her. His hands smothered her hips, lifting her slightly and then setting her down to blissfully envelop his broad length. He contemplated taunting her again as he had earlier—asking if this was all she wanted. He didn't care that it was. The arrogant side of his demeanor, which he'd only privately admit was more potent than he cared for, promised she'd be wanting more before all was said and done.

Kale took pleasure in the way Davia honored him with her throaty cries—loud and unabashed. She met his thrusts and reached back to rake her nails across his thighs as he took her with greater ferocity. When it occurred to him that he might be a bit rough with her, her fingernails dug into his thighs, ordering him not to think about stopping. He didn't, and their time together passed in a hypnotic blur of ecstasy.

"Come back with me," he told her much later.

They'd collapsed to the lounge floor. Outside, the snow was coming down in blinding sheets that blanketed the land in a thick, untouched wave of white.

Kale lay on his stomach on the rug in front of the fire where they'd catnapped after crawling there from the window. Davia rested on his back, her body a seductive covering for his.

His slurred tone brought a smile to her face and made her want to tease him. "Well, I'm not a mogul like you and can't afford to take too much time off, so…it makes more sense for you to just come on back with me."

"All right."

He spoke without hesitation. His tone instantly telling Davia that he hadn't been teasing at all.

Kale laughed when she remained unresponsive to his decision. "Are we done playing now?" he asked.

"Don't you mean am *I* done playing now?"

"All right." Again his reply came without hesitation.

Davia pressed her face between his shoulder blades and inhaled. The scent of soap and sweat made for an intoxicating aroma she wished to commit to memory. She looked up when Kale's voice began to vibrate through his body.

"Do you remember what I said to you in your office about women always giving me what I want without me having to do anything?"

"Yeah." Davia offered her response quietly.

"Remember me saying that somewhere along the way I guessed I started having a problem with it?"

"Yes." Her response was even softer that time.

"Would it surprise you to know I didn't realize how big a problem I had with it until I talked to you in your office that day?"

Her teasing manner then revisited. "So you had two epiphanies that day. Deciding I was the only one you could sell to and now this."

Kale had to grin. "Those thoughtful listening skills again." He sighed and then turned to stare at the calming fire. "I think that happened because I'd never been surprised before. Not like that."

Davia didn't know if he could tell how rigid she'd become, and she didn't argue when he changed their resting positions, putting her beneath him to look down at her.

"I came to your office to see if you were as gorgeous as I thought you were in that picture and for all the reasons I told you I had, but I didn't tell you how much you surprised me." He reached out to smooth back a few of the clipped tendrils from her forehead and then rested his fist back against his cheek.

"I'm sure there was a lot more than met the eye to so many of the women I've known," he said as he shrugged. "I just never bothered or wanted to bother to take a look. And then you came in handling business on your headset and I was... I was hooked." His brows joined in a bewildered frown. "How is that possible?"

Davia emerged from her rigid state. "There was a lot more going on between us before we ever even met—

with your uncle, my aunt, Tella. Maybe you're getting all that mixed up into thinking we were…meant to be something more." She resisted biting her lip as she studied him, wondering how he'd react to her claim.

He nodded for a moment, as if to consider her words. "Is that why you slept with me? Just giving in to drama already at work between us and getting it…mixed up with meaning we were meant to be…this?" For emphasis, he scanned the length of her body lying alongside his.

She didn't follow his gaze. Rather, kept her eyes fixed on his stunning face. "I slept with you because I wanted to give in to what I wanted. I guess I'm no different than any of the other women who fall at your feet, Kale. There's nothing surprising here."

He gave a smile that didn't reach his dazzling eyes by a long shot. Offering no counter or confirmation to her opinion, he merely pushed to his feet and offered her his hand.

"We won't be able to walk if we stay on this floor much longer. Come on, I'll take you back to your room."

Davia accepted his extended hand, but hesitantly. She had no problem with spending the night on the floor if he was there with her. Sadly, that time had passed. Quietly, they collected their things. Davia slipped into her jumper and opted to carry the rest of her things. In minutes they were at her door.

"Good night, Davi," he was saying just as she crossed into the suite.

He walked away and she followed his departure

with sad eyes before she closed the door. Resting back against it, Davia let her belongings drop to the floor and hid her face in her hands.

Chapter 13

The next several days were like a storm cloud of activity. Kale and Davia tended to matters pertaining to their own personal businesses. All this, while everyone worked diligently to put into action Kale's idea for moving forward with the hoped-for land development plans.

The Waverlys devoted half of Barrett's large study into a workspace for their guests.

Kale and Davia were most grateful as the guest lounge had proved to be too tempting a space to keep their minds on work.

Work consisted of scouring through the old news clippings and photos the innkeepers had collected. It seemed that almost every town resident who could trace their families back three generations or more was represented in the Mullins history stuffing the big accordion folders.

Kale spent his time getting to know town officials who could be responsible for green-lighting the hoped-for building permits. Meanwhile, Davia and Estelle took it upon themselves to have the photos scanned for copies.

Thanks to bar owners Troy and Rich Ayers, Davia and Estelle were able to share many of those photos with the town residents. The Ayers brothers had confirmed Estelle's selections of who would be most open to receiving the pictures of their parents at work on Chase Waverly's dream of bringing the movies to Mullins.

Barry took charge of dispersing the photos to his fellow council members. He didn't use as much tact as Davia and Estelle, but shared the photos with everyone who was represented among his council colleagues. He did this regardless of their stance on the theater project.

This included Mitchell Barns. Barry regaled his wife and their inn guests with the story of how speechless Mitch Barns was upon receiving the photo of his father as a boy. Shepard Barns Jr. stood high atop a ladder being supported by Kale's uncle Bryant. The boy grinned wildly while affixing the letters to a giant marquee that proclaimed the theater would be coming that summer.

Davia decided to enjoy her breakfast that morning in Barrett's study, reviewing more of the photos and clippings. She was about to break off another chunk of the soft wheat bagel when she saw there were more than photos among the news clippings. There were also blueprints.

She was marveling over the collection she'd just unearthed when a single knock turned her attention to the study doorway.

"Morning." Her greeting was cheerful when she found Kale standing just inside the room. "Hope you're in the mood for breakfast, because Estelle outdid herself today."

On top of everything else on the spread were the homemade bagels. Davia didn't think she'd ever met anyone who made bagels from scratch. The creations were light, flavorful and irresistible. Davia hadn't even realized she'd forgotten to add cream cheese until she was halfway done.

"Estelle's making me a fresh pot of coffee to go along with my breakfast, so…" Kale eased his hands into the pockets of the olive-green carpenters' pants he wore. "She told me you were in here," he said.

"You'll never guess what I found." Davia waved him over. "Take a look at all these blueprints I came across. They've got to be for the original theater."

Kale approached as Davia had urged, but he clearly had no real interest just then in the blueprints. He fingered a couple of the midnight-blue sheets displaying the white print outlining the construction and then nudged them aside.

"I make you think about her, don't I? About Tella?" His gaze was still fixed on the prints.

Davia's excitement over her unexpected discovery waned.

"What I can't figure," Kale was saying as he eased a hip down on the worktable set at the far end of the room, "is whether you're thinking of how you misunderstood my intentions or the consequences my actions brought about. I know one of them is why you're afraid."

Davia turned to him suddenly, looking as though she were about to dispute his words.

"You are, aren't you?" he probed. "You're afraid." There was no criticism in his words, only knowing. "Afraid to give this a chance," he finished.

Davia's laughter was sharp, nervous. "Are you hearing yourself? We live on opposite sides of the country, remember?"

"And I don't give a damn about that." Kale almost growled the words. He closed his eyes, appearing as though he wished to summon calm. "If I have my way, Davia, it won't be that way forever," he said when he opened them.

His deep, coaxing stare drifted down her body as he spoke and caused Davia to swallow hard before she averted her face from his. There was a knock echoing in the room then, breaking the tense moment.

"Hey, guys, sorry for interrupting," Estelle was saying.

"No problem, Estelle. What's up?"

Kale made the save while Davia took a few moments to collect herself before she turned to her hostess. Estelle had arrived with a petite brunette who wore her short hair in a straight pageboy cut that framed her round, pretty face.

"This is Sheila Barns. She's Mitchell Barns's wife," Estelle said by way of introduction.

"I apologize for barging in so early in the morning," Sheila Barns was saying once Kale and Davia had greeted her with smiles and handshakes.

"Can we get you anything, Mrs. Barns?" Davia asked.

"Yeah, Sheila. I just put on a fresh pot of coffee," Estelle added.

Sheila was already waving a hand. "No, no, thank you both."

"Will you have a seat, Mrs. Barns?" Kale said.

"Oh, uh, no...no. But thank you." Sheila declined Kale's offer but graced him with a shy smile and a look tinged with a hint of awe.

The woman's awestruck look was soon shifting to the far side of the study where Kale and Davia had set up shop. Two large-screen monitors presented the photos that Davia and Estelle had scanned so far. They played in a continuous slide show.

On slow steps, Sheila Barns moved closer to the display. "I was wondering whether there were any more pictures of the kids working on the theater?"

Quick, excited laughter chirped past Sheila's lips as she pointed at another picture that flashed on the screen. Hands clasped, she turned, grinning as though she was thoroughly delighted.

"Mitch hasn't been able to stop looking at that picture of his dad helping with the marquee since Barry gave it to him a few days ago," Sheila explained. "He doesn't talk much about his dad, but when he does..." A little of the excitement dimmed in her eyes.

"I always got the feeling that a lot of things went unsaid between them." Sheila began to walk the quiet room. "There've been times I've been with both of them before my father-in-law passed and I... I got the feeling it wasn't just things unsaid on Mitch's part but on his dad's, too. Two men set in their ways and too proud to change or even admit they were acting stupidly." Sheila sighed as though realizing how she'd gone on. She sent a refreshed smile toward Estelle, Davia and Kale.

"Mitch already framed the picture and has a copy of it on his desk at the office."

"Aw, Sheila, we're glad he got a kick out of it," Estelle said, her smile bright.

Sheila pointed back across her shoulder. "I just saw another one on the screen I know he'd be thrilled to have."

"We'll get it for you, and any others we find," Davia promised.

"Thank you. Thank you both." Sheila gave a vibrant nod. "Um, Estelle has all my contact info, so…"

"We'll check through everything else we've got and send whatever we find right away," Kale softly answered.

Sheila sent Kale another awed smile and then was backing toward the study door. "I'll just let you get back to work." She looked to Estelle and put a hand through the bend of the woman's arm as they turned to leave.

"Kale, the coffee should be done. You can help yourself while I walk Sheila to the door," Estelle instructed.

Alone, Kale and Davia stood silently enjoying the moment they'd just experienced.

"It was a very good idea," Davia complimented him, watching as Kale survey their workspace.

"I guess all that still remains to be seen." He gave a good-natured sigh and shrugged beneath the lightweight sweatshirt he wore. "Guess I'll go grab that coffee."

"You were right," Davia called when he was at the door. "You do make me think of Tella, but not for either of the reasons you mentioned—not because of the consequences of your actions or even because of my misunderstanding about your intentions." She began to pace the study as Sheila Barns had done moments earlier.

"I meant it when I said I believed you. I'm glad you were there for my friend that day. When I think of Tella... Kale, I think of *my* intentions and how weak they were. Had my own intentions been stronger, had I been more insistent with her, told her how it was going to be and that was that—"

"Davia, don't." Kale had turned away from the door.

But Davia kept talking. "Maybe she would've gotten the help she needed."

"Davia." His rich voice was firmer when he called out to her that time.

Undaunted, she continued. "If I'd done that, maybe she wouldn't have killed herself."

Kale caught Davia's shoulders and gave her a slight shake that he hoped would get her to snap to. "Please tell me you haven't been blaming yourself all this time for what happened to Martella," he said when her eyes met his.

"No, Kale." She fixed him with a miserable smile. "All this time, I've been blaming *you*, hating you for the advantage I thought you'd taken of her." She shook her head, pulling a hand back through her cropped hair. "I think I always knew that was just an excuse—a smoke screen to hide the truth from myself.

"Once I had the truth from you about what happened between you guys, that smoke screen evaporated and forced me to see the reality of it."

"Which was?" Kale's query went unanswered for a

moment. "What, Davia? That what happened to Martella was somehow your fault?"

"That I should have, could have, done more. I approached her troubles with a *business* solution, Kale."

"So did I, babe."

"But you weren't her best friend. She wasn't a sister to you."

He nodded in acknowledgment, his tone softer when he spoke again. "Ask yourself this, then. Would Martella want her best friend—her sister—blaming herself for a decision she made? A terrible decision, true, but one *she* made? Think about that." He put a hard kiss to her forehead and then he was gone.

Chapter 14

Kale and Davia put their total focus on the project then. There were lingering legal issues involving the property that proved to be hectic but also provided a welcome distraction from talk of the past.

Preoccupied by so much, they had left little time for such conversations anyway. When they weren't meeting about the land, Davia divided her time between visits to Estelle Waverly's boutique and the Ayerses' pub, where she reviewed the decades-old blueprints of the unrealized theater. Additionally, she weighed the fruits of her own research and sketched out her ideal image of the envisioned project.

Kale had done his own research, as well, and spent his time reviewing those findings. He also took meetings with would-be members of a possible construction crew in anticipation of hope becoming reality.

It was after one such meeting when, deep in thought, he was startled by a greeting.

"Good morning."

Kale looked up from the table he occupied near the hearth of the town café. "Uh…good morning." He gave a slow shake of his head and appeared confused. "Sorry, I almost forgot what your voice sounded like. How long's it been since we talked? I was sure we'd be sitting down to our first movie in the new theater before we spoke to each other again. Or…before *you* spoke to *me* again."

Davia accepted the dig without argument. Folding her arms over her chest, she rested her thigh against Kale's table and smiled coolly. "Is that why you left this at my door?" Onto the table she dropped a sheaf of photos wrapped in a clear protective sleeve.

"What do you mean?" Kale barely spared the photos a glance. His expression remained innocent.

"A little something to spark conversation, maybe?" Davia prodded.

Kale leaned over the table to peer down at what Davia had dropped there. "And what sort of conversation could this spark?" he asked.

Davia's huff was as throaty as her voice. "Please tell me you meant this as a joke."

Kale considered the pictures again and then looked to Davia. "Why would you think that? Do they make you want to laugh?"

"Laughing would be better than cringing, which was my initial reaction."

"Well, I can't see why they'd make anyone cringe."

"You wouldn't." Ire still colored Davia's voice. "You

can't be thinking this is the kind of place these people would want here?"

Photos covered the paperwork Kale had been studying when Davia arrived. All featured glossy depictions of dazzling multiplex theaters. Some had been fashioned for malls, others occupied space inside skyscrapers. All were past projects that Kale had had a hand in.

"Kale, you can't possibly be thinking this is the kind of thing that would be right for Mullins." Davia's tone had sobered somewhat, but the patient chord was still strained.

Kale selected one of the glossies to study a bit more closely. "I got nothing but rave reviews on this spot," he mused blandly before fixing on another. "Humph. This one, too. They're all very profitable. This one in particular..." he said as he gestured to the photo he held. "It added to the allure of the mall, leading to increased visits from town residents as well as those who lived outside it."

"Kale, Mullins has no malls." Davia shook her head even as she smiled. "The town residents you're talking about actually live in cities that can accommodate three or more multiplexes this size."

Kale shook his head. "I don't think you're giving this town the benefit of the doubt."

"Are you serious?" Davia's throaty laugh harbored on sounding boisterous. "The parking lot alone would eat up most of our acreage."

"Well, I'm sure folks wouldn't mind parking outside of town." Kale peppered his statement with a lackadaisical shrug. "We could even provide carriage rides to the theater."

"Kale!" In that moment Davia couldn't be sure if he was serious or not. Eyes narrowing, she glared down and decided to wait him out.

Moments later they were both dissolving into waves of laughter.

"I'll bet that felt good," Kale said when the mood mellowed around them.

Davia thumbed a laugh tear from her eye. "Is that why you said it?"

He gave her a rakish smile. "I thought you could use a laugh."

Davia finally took a seat at the table. Propping her palm to her cheek, she sighed. "I'm sorry, Kale, I didn't mean to shut you out that way."

"Don't apologize to me." He nudged the photos. "I did that for your sake, not mine. Blaming yourself for Martella is the last thing you should be doing."

"I know and I…I wasn't. I didn't think I was… Guess it hadn't occurred to me that I was doing exactly that until I met you and the idea of her was right there at the very tip top of my mind instead of tucked away in that private place I have reserved for her—for all the things I haven't dealt with."

"How much have you got in that private place?" he asked her.

Davia shook her head warily. "I think—I *hope*—Tella's the last of it."

"Don't you think it's time you closed that place for good?"

"I definitely think it's time." Davia settled back on the chair in an exaggerated fashion even as she favored him with an easy smile. "Thank you."

Kale half shrugged. "That's what friends are for. It's a shame I want more than your friendship."

Davia fought not to bristle over the second half of his statement. He was talking again before she could speak to it.

"I guess I had some unfinished issues when it came to Martella, too." He returned her easy smile. "Thanks for being the catalyst I needed to face them."

Davia thought of reciprocating his "that's what friends are for" line, but she wasn't sure how well it would be received.

That evening Davia decided to brave the bitter outdoor temps when she ventured to the inn's rooftop. She'd been curious about the view from that spot since Barry's mention of it when she and Kale had first arrived at the bed-and-breakfast.

It was approaching 4:00 p.m. The sun had not yet set, but with the ever-present snow clouds lingering above, a heavier darkness loomed. The remaining light accentuated the brilliant white snow that blanketed every inch of the environment.

Barrett Waverly was right to be so long-winded with his boasts, Davia thought. The scene from the rooftop was unreal, otherworldly. She could have stayed there forever if it weren't so damned cold. Or if she had something besides her coat to keep her warm.

Like Kale Asante.

As if her thought had conjured him, Davia turned from the snow-dusted brick railing and Kale was standing just a few feet away from the roof's access door.

"Sorry for bothering you." His voice seemed to echo against the still air.

Davia gave a quick shake of her head. "You aren't. I, um…" She waved a hand behind her. "I only came up to see if the view was as good as Barrett said."

"And?"

"He didn't lie."

Kale came to stand near the railing and take in the view, as well. "No, he didn't," he agreed and then said nothing further. But for the faint cry of the wind, silence settled between them.

"Barrett's sure there won't be another meeting for a few days," Kale was saying, his voice once again carrying over the quiet cold. "I thought maybe we could take some time to continue our conversation from the café. Maybe even tack on a field trip."

The idea had Davia turning away from the view to regard him curiously.

Kale didn't need a verbal prompt. "You up for seeing some spots in person instead of online?" he asked.

Davia tilted her head curiously. "What have you got in mind?"

"Do you know anything about the Xyler Chronicles?"

Davia gasped before a smile spread across her face. "Are you a fan, too?"

It was Kale's turn to gape. "You know it?"

Davia threw back her head. "Are you kidding? I've been in love with the franchise for years. I've got all the movies on DVD. The fifth one is due out this summer."

Kale shook his head and chuckled. "I would've never pegged you for an action-movie junkie."

"What?" Playful bewilderment crept into Davia's

light eyes. "Didn't my preference for beer give me away?"

Laughter edged in to warm the air for a moment, but when Davia shivered, Kale wasted no time pulling her back against him.

Oh, yes, she thought. Now she had everything she needed to enjoy the view forever.

"So do you think the new Xyler will be a good one?" Kale asked once Davia was snug against him.

"I hope so." She closed her eyes against the stunning view and took her pleasure in absorbing the feel of Kale surrounding her. "They've got lots of work to do if they plan on it being better or as good as the last one. Guess I'll find out when it releases."

"How'd you like to go to the premiere?"

"Kale Asante, is that an invitation?" Something sly and playful hugged her voice.

"Could be." He drew her tighter against him. "The premiere's scheduled to be at one of my theaters next weekend."

Floored, Davia made a brisk turn in his arms. "Are you serious?"

"Very." Something mysterious hid behind the word. "There *is* a condition, though."

"And that is?"

"The premiere's in Miami and you'd have to stay with me while we're there."

She swallowed in reflex but was otherwise cool. "Any reason for that?"

"Damn right there is." His tone was as easy as his manner when he turned her into his kiss.

Davia revised her earlier remark about the view then.

Having Kale join her wasn't all she needed to enjoy it forever. *This*—his kiss—was all she needed. The snow began to drift downward at a steadier pace. The temperature had dipped, but the fact held no sway over the lovers.

The kiss possessed all the steam and heat that had so far epitomized their encounters.

"Is that the reason? So you can kiss me?" She panted once he finally let her take in air.

Propping an index finger beneath her chin, Kale tipped back her head as if to prepare her to take another kiss. "Among other things, Ms. Sands," he said. "Among other things."

Chapter 15

Miami, Florida

Kale's home was all that Davia expected and much of what she didn't expect. The chic and refined qualities were ones she agreed were well earned, but the warm and homey touches were a definite surprise.

Upon arrival, there was, of course, the unmistakable impression of wealth and elegance. Davia's jaw dropped when the car rolled past the white-iron fence beyond the security booth.

Kale, who was working at his phone, noticed Davia scooting closer to the window on her side of the chauffeured car. He forgot the phone, preferring to observe her reaction to the place he'd called home for the last six years.

Intrigued and impressed, Davia scanned the grounds that were awash in late-afternoon sun. As the car rounded the circular drive with its centerpiece of towering palms, she could see the edges of an in-ground swimming pool in the rear of the property. Beyond it, a smaller pool sat in its own raised-platform gazebo. The house itself was a multistory construction in Coral Gables. The Mediterranean-style estate had a mesmerizing view of Biscayne Bay and the serenity of the view was awe inspiring.

Davia shook her head in wonder. "This place would make a great inn for Barrett and Estelle," she mused.

Kale blinked, a brief frown tugging at the sleek lines of his brow. "You don't approve?"

Davia still eyed the estate. "No, I think it's gorgeous."

"But you don't approve?" he persisted.

"That depends on how many people live here with you." Davia flashed him a teasing smile across her shoulder before she turned to take in more of the view. She'd meant her words as a tease, never realizing how much the man at her side cared about what she thought.

"No, no roommates." Kale sighed. "This is all for me," he said as the car pulled to a stop in the circular redbrick driveway.

Davia didn't wait for the chauffeur to escort her, but left the car under her own steam. She was eager to begin her tour of the place.

"It's all right, Jerry." Kale sent the driver an easy wave and went to where Davia stood looking up at the glorious azure sky. She stood with her face turned toward the sun and smiled when she looked over at Kale.

"Been missing the sun?" he guessed.

Davia shrugged. "What can I say? I'm a Cali girl at heart, but I *will* admit that I think I could survive without year-round sun."

Kale moved closer, nudged her arm with his elbow. "But it doesn't hurt sometimes, does it?"

"No." She turned her face back up to the sky. "It doesn't hurt at all."

When Kale touched her arm again, it was to turn her toward the wide semicircular steps leading up to the front door. "Show you inside?" he asked as he offered his hand.

Davia obliged and soon they'd cleared the entrance staircase and were strolling the gleaming black-and-mocha checkerboard floor of a large foyer that opened into a bright, airy living room. The area was expansive and finished in shades of cream and gold. Large, healthy plants occupied space in wide brass urns that claimed opposing corners of the room. Persian rugs complimented the color scheme of the walls and plush seating graced the polished marble flooring.

Kale kept a measurable distance from Davia once they entered the room. He followed her quietly as she strolled his home looking up and all around like she was a kid taking in her first museum. Once she'd covered much of the main level, she found the stairway and began her tour of the next floor, which consisted of a well-equipped gaming room, gym and mini den.

By the time she'd gone through a few of his home's nine bedrooms, Kale admitted to himself that he was more than a little eager to know what she thought.

"So?" he probed when she finally came to a stop and

was leaning against the doorjamb to the lounge at the end of the bedroom wing.

Davia's manner was playfully nonchalant. "Splashy on the outside, cozy on the inside. How'd you manage that?"

Kale felt some of his apprehension ease. "Does that mean you haven't lost all respect for me?"

Davia shrugged. "The warmth of your home is a redeeming quality…so, no, I haven't lost *all* respect for you, but I'll save my final opinion till after I've gotten a taste of your hospitality skills."

Kale left the scoop, swivel chair he'd occupied and came to where she stood inside the doorway. In one, fluid move he had her tight against his chest. "My hospitality is the best part about being at my house."

"In what way?" She smoothed the backs of her hands across his cheeks. She felt no need to cling to him for support. She felt completely secure in his arms. She was gasping a second later when his perfect teeth latched onto her earlobe, assaulting the tender flesh with a painfully sweet suckle that caused her to shiver.

"To answer that, I'd have to show you to another room."

Davia leaned in to him. "I thought I'd seen almost every room."

"Almost." He abandoned her earlobe and made his way down her neck. "Stop talking to me and kiss me," he ordered in a pretend huff.

She complied.

The act started off lusty and amplified from there. Davia threaded her fingers through Kale's close curls and shivered then, as much from the feel of his hair under her fingertips as she did from the sensation of his tongue plundering her mouth with thunderous determination.

Eventually she moved her fingers from Kale's hair to curl them into his shirt collar as he carried her easily down the corridor beyond the rooms she had just toured. Kale rounded the long hall en route to a set of towering double doors that proved to be their final destination. The master bedroom.

Beyond those doors, the couple made speedy work of shedding their clothes. Pieces either drifted to the floor or were flung clear across the room. When they stood in front of one another at last naked, they took but a breadth of time to drink in the sight of one another. Then he lifted her into his arms.

He ascended the few stairs of the brief platform to his bed and lay her on the mattress. Then he followed her down, breaking their intense kiss only to lavish Davia's body with more of the same.

She arched into every glide of his lips each time his tongue treated her skin to a lengthy bathing. When Kale favored her sex with one of those deep kisses, Davia arched into the most perfect bow and shuddered his name. She expected more of the same when he made his way back up the length of her body. She wanted more of his tongue's extraordinary skill.

Kale had other ideas, however. He took a condom from one of the unfinished wooden night tables then began making his way down her body to treat her with more of the lavish kisses. He was undoubtedly prepared when he finally covered her and claimed her the moment his body aligned with hers.

Davia's hunger for him reached ravenous proportions within seconds of him seating himself to the hilt inside her. With one thrust she threw back her head and sobbed out her delight.

The night was lengthy and sensuous. And everything she'd hoped for.

Davia was at work the next morning, manning two of the six burners on the pristine chrome stove in Kale's kitchen. There, she watched over an iron skillet of plump pancakes and one that sizzled with slices of fragrant bacon. She smiled and gave in to a faint shiver when Kale's arms eased around her waist as he drew her back against him.

"I appreciate you going to all this trouble but you didn't have to cook for me." He spoke into her hair.

Davia gave the pancakes one final turn. "Can't have you accusing me of not being a proper houseguest, can I?"

Something in her tone gave Kale pause, for he eased back just a fraction yet kept her trapped in the small prison his hands made on either side of her.

"Did I overstep by bringing you here, Davi?" he asked after the passing of a few silent moments.

Davia stilled her work at the stove. "Why would you think that?"

"We really don't know each other well enough for me to have you here alone and at my mercy, do we?"

Davia removed the bacon from the stove and began to move the pancakes to a warming plate. "Have you got anything in mind that would require me to need your mercy?" she asked.

Kale drew his nose across Davia's nape and nuzzled her there. "I did go a little easy on you last night."

"Such a shame. Had I known that, I'd have urged you against it."

"Urged me, huh?"

Davia lost her interest in the food and was snuggling back into their lovers embrace. She savored the sensations Kale sent rushing through her body as one hand cupped a breast beneath the silk robe she sported. He began a delicious thumb massage through the material. Its twin was subjected to a slow, thorough squeeze. In seconds, Davia was panting.

"I take it you can't wait until after breakfast?"

Kale was at work on her earlobe, suckling and kissing. "If you wanted to spend your time cooking, I wouldn't have brought you here."

"Really? So...where, then?"

"Hell, we could've stayed in Iowa. You could've cooked at the inn to give Estelle a break from all that kitchen work."

Davia laughed but was soon sobering as she observed her surroundings. "I think it'd be hard for anyone to come into a kitchen like this and not want to cook at least one meal."

"I'll remember that next time."

Davia recovered quickly from the momentary tension roused by his words. Her recovery sadly wasn't fast enough to escape Kale's notice. Silently, he decided not to follow along the line of conversation her response begged.

It was just as well, for Davia had another topic of discussion she wanted to investigate just then. She made a move to free herself from Kale's prison, smiling when he granted her release.

"How'd you find out I was the one who started the rumor about you and Tella?" She set the food onto the wide bar top lining the cooking island while she waited on his response.

"Does it matter?" On slow steps, Kale made his way around the island.

"Guess not. I mean, the damage is already done." Davia went to grab plates and eating utensils. "I'd like to know, anyway, though."

It was true. She wanted to know. But she couldn't admit that she wanted to avert whatever conversation was about to take place following his mention of a return trip to his home.

"I found out when I almost lost out on a deal." Kale took his place at the island and started preparing his plate. "It was a land purchase deal I was hoping to close shortly after…what happened with Martella."

Davia prepped her plate, as well, though her movements gradually slowed as she fixed on Kale's explanation.

"The owner's wife was…unhappy about us doing business together. The news was disappointing." Kale added maple syrup to the side of his plate instead of dousing the pancakes. "It wasn't the first time a husband and wife team didn't see eye to eye and I wasn't about to be responsible for the guy falling out with his wife. I was ready to let it go when the guy told me his wife didn't just have an issue with us doing business but with us also being friends. I'd known him since grad school." Kale shook his head while breaking a strip of bacon in two. "Anyway, that's when we both figured it'd probably be a good idea to find out what was at the bottom of it."

Davia had her plate filled but couldn't rouse the energy to dive into the meal.

"Thankfully we all knew each other long enough, so she felt comfortable talking to me when I pressed the issue. Evan and Sonya Mayes?" He looked to Davia then. "Sonya says you and she are friends."

Davia forced a nod. "Yes. I, uh… I've known Sonya for years."

"Well, she was the one who told me how…unhappy you were with me." Kale chewed the piece of bacon. "I explained what really happened, and I told Sonya it was possible that you had no idea of the truth. I didn't need them to tell me I'd most likely have to repeat the story to others." He smiled an ill-humored smile. "I already told you why I hadn't been interested in doing that at the time."

Davia looked as though she'd lost her appetite for the delicious-looking breakfast. "I've made a real mess, haven't I?"

Kale swallowed the bacon and reached for another slice. "You had your reasons."

"Doesn't excuse what I did. I took one look at you and just—"

"Assumed," Kale said with a smirk, recalling their previous conversation on the matter when they were en route to Iowa. "Would've been good if we could've met and hashed all this out before now."

"I think it happened when it was supposed to." Davia finally felt up to cutting into the hot, fluffy stack of pancakes. "Any sooner and I may not have been able to hear you."

"And so here we are," Kale taunted.

"And so here we are," Davia agreed, finding comfort in the idea she carried hope there was a chance they could be more.

Chapter 16

The day was, of course, a glorious one that captured everything one thought of when Miami weather was the topic of discussion.

Kale and Davia made quick work of showering and dressing following breakfast. The day was slated to be one of sightseeing mixed with business. Kale wanted to show Davia some of his favorite movie houses—ones he hoped to bring in just a touch of for their Iowa project.

Likewise, Davia made note of a few houses she was interested in visiting. Kale was both stunned and impressed by her knowledge of his town. Additionally, he was more than a little peeved to learn she'd spent so much time there and within his reach without him being aware of her presence. Missed opportunities were definitely not among his favorite things.

It was no surprise that Kale's choices for his part of the sightseeing outing were among the biggest and splashiest of the Miami film scene. While Davia didn't think any were appropriate for the Iowa locale, she couldn't help but admire Kale's eye for detail.

More than that, she could see that for all the flash and dazzle of the stunning multiplexes they visited, there was an obvious sense of warmth that managed to thrive in the midst of all the opulence. She didn't tell him so, but Davia was quite certain her unlikely partner would bring the same attention of warmth and welcome to a project of a smaller scale.

The day wrapped up with time spent off the beaten path when they took in a few dinner theaters in the area. Kale was shocked to learn that she'd been responsible for them and for many of the more quaint locales they'd visited that day.

He was once again reflecting on missed opportunities by the time they'd returned to his home to get dressed for the evening's movie premiere. The discovery that Davia had worked the jobs they'd visited before everything that happened with Tella gnawed at some new place inside him.

"You know, I never get romantically involved with folks in our profession." Though her words were true, Davia offered them in a teasing fashion while she smoothed invisible wrinkles from her gown. She didn't realize how seriously the man on the other side of the bedroom was taking her words.

"I remember you saying that you'd give it all up for something that was really worth it." Kale spoke absently while surveying the tux he'd laid out on the bed.

Teasing losing its sheen, Davia turned to him with curiosity welling in her eyes. "Kale, does it seriously not matter to you at all that the only reason we came into each other's lives is because of an inheritance—and one we don't even know if we'll be able to do anything with if Mitch Barns and his other like-minded Mullinsers have their way?" She left the walk-in closet where Kale had insisted she put her things. "My point is, if not for the inheritance, we'd have never met each other."

"And because of that you don't trust what we have. Don't trust me."

"Kale…"

He pulled her close and put a kiss to her temple. "I understand, Davi."

When he left the room, Davia hung her head. "No, Kale…no, you don't."

The premiere of the fifth installment of the Xyler Chronicles was slated to be an over-the-top event and those rumors had not been exaggerated in the least.

Kale and Davia were arriving on the red carpet around six that evening. The glitter and glamour appealed to all in its midst, especially to the swarms of eager fans hoping to catch a glimpse of the celebs in attendance. Of course, the movie's popular stars were at the top of that list. The paparazzi were in full gear with cameras of all shapes and scopes ready to immortalize the images of the stunningly dressed members of the audience filing into the theater. The sun was the perfect finishing touch to set the scene in elusive brilliance. It was starting its descent, which had the city lights beginning their nightly illumination.

Davia was as amazed as a child viewing something she'd only dreamed of as she took in the allure of the elegant multiplex she and Kale had visited that morning. At that moment and in all its bedazzled beauty, the structure was quite a sight. "This is incredible." She clutched Kale's arm with a bit more urgency while breathing out the compliment.

"It sure is."

Davia believed Kale's response was made in carnest, though it was clear to her that he was preoccupied. They hadn't spoken much more since the scene back at the house while they were dressing. She was desperate to make amends, though she knew the only way to do that was to be totally honest herself. How was she to do that with Kale? Davia wondered, when she hadn't figured out how to do that with herself.

They were met by a broadly muscled man with smiling amber eyes who had rushed forward to take Kale's hand in a hearty shake. However distant Kale had seemed, none of it showed when he launched into introductions.

"Davia, this is my chief architect and a guy who's known me since we were both in diapers, Lyle Neese. Lyle, this is Davia Sands. My partner in the inheritance from Uncle Bry," Kale explained.

"It's a pleasure, Mr. Neese." Davia spoke through her smile.

"The pleasure is all mine, Ms. Sands. And, please, call me Lyle."

She responded with an easy nod. "Thanks—and it's Davia."

Lyle enveloped Davia's hand in both of his. "Lovely name for a lovely lady." He studied her face as though committing her features to memory. "It's so great to have you here." He regarded Davia for a few seconds more before he turned back to Kale. "You'll find the escort to your seats waiting just inside. He should be holding up a name card to get your attention." Lyle clapped Kale's shoulder and then moved on.

"Someone's excited," Davia remarked, feeling her own anticipation for the evening approach Lyle's obvious demeanor.

"It's no surprise," Kale said as he watched his friend disappear into the heavy crowd. "No one can say Lyle isn't dedicated and passionate about his work. Especially on nights like this." Kale paused to scan the circus-like intensity. "He's like a kid whenever there's talk in the air about some premiere being held at one of our venues."

"Well, his excitement is contagious and I don't think I need any more help being excited."

Davia had been to a few movie premieres in her day, but never anything quite like what she stood in the midst of. Silently she gave thanks that Estelle Waverly, in addition to being an innkeeper, was a damn fine boutique owner. Davia had already added several to-die-for pieces to her wardrobe, courtesy of Estelle's and the gown she'd selected for that evening's event was no exception.

Not only did the pearl tone of the gown complement the champagne color of Kale's tux, it added an even more dewy allure to Davia's dark complexion. Matching open-toed pumps peeked out from a scalloped hemline that almost dragged the carpet. The shoes added several inches to her noticeable height while calling attention to her willowy form and its subtle yet beckoning host of curves.

The gown's halter bodice drew the eye to her bare back and shoulders before it cinched tightly at the small of her back. There, Kale's hand rested between intermittent bouts of dancing along her spine. The gestures were subconscious yet effective displays of possession.

"Lyle loves this stuff but that's not why he's so excited," Kale was saying as he and Davia neared the multiplex lobby.

"What's his excuse?" Davia playfully inquired, enjoying the lighthearted sensation that could've taken her off her feet.

"He's so excited because I once told him the only woman I'd ever bring to one of these things is the woman I intend to marry." With that, Kale moved on to shake hands with someone who'd just greeted him.

Davia was barely able to put one foot in front of the other, nor could she swallow around the lump that had found its way to the base of her throat.

The Xyler Chronicles V: Stealth Capture lived up to all its hype and then some. The South Beach Array proved to be the perfect venue. Every explosion, gun battle and car chase was effectively presented and heard in the tri-level state-of-the-art theater.

There wasn't a bad seat in the place, literally. Besides being perfectly positioned, the seats were thick, deep armchairs that offered maximum comfort. Davia had an excellent time, despite the fact that every romantic moment shared between the film's hero Dex Xyler and his leading lady Chelsea Minx only took her thoughts back to Kale. And the words he'd uttered just before they headed into the theater.

...the woman I intend to marry.

The premiere wrapped and another trip down the red carpet was needed for film reactions and photo ops. Afterward, Kale and Davia were whisked away to a club on the penthouse level of a skyscraper where a well-attended party was in full swing. It took Kale and Davia at least twenty minutes to make their way across the room, because Kale was called in myriad directions for handshakes and more photos.

Davia didn't mind being the man's arm candy, but it was an added bonus when she garnered her own share of attention from business acquaintances she hadn't expected to see. The evening was pretty much perfect, especially when she had the chance for her own photo op with Xyler Chronicles's leading man, Coyt Vincent.

And then came the dancing.

"I hope this was all worth the money you spent on the new dress," Kale was saying later when he held her as they danced to a slow song.

"Are you serious? Tonight has been sooo worth it." Davia beamed. There'd been times she'd had to steel herself from jumping in place over all the exciting aspects of the evening.

Kale reached for the champagne glass Davia held while they danced. Each had sipped from a single flute while swaying to the jazzy instrumental.

"I still don't think we've done all that we set out to

do," he mused once he'd handed the glass back to Davia and eased his hands back around her waist.

"I think we accomplished a lot. You know what I like. I know what you like."

"I suppose that's true." Kale's gaze intensified the longer he watched her. "What I like goes far beyond a movie theater, Davia."

She finished off the champagne. "Kale, um, I'm sorry that I… I just can't seem to say more about what I want for us and I—"

He dipped his head, suddenly and effectively silencing her. "I don't expect you to say anything *now*. But I *want* you to—when you're ready." He followed with a wink and smile, giving her a quick nod when she reciprocated the gesture, and then put a kiss to her forehead.

"I know we have a strange situation here, Davi. It's not following the normal route things like this are supposed to take. At least, I don't *think* this is the route it's supposed to take." He shrugged but faintly. "Guess I've been in enough wrong situations to know when a right one hits me."

"And I can't believe you think I'm a *right* one with the unbelievable amount of angst I'm carrying around." Davia gave a short laugh in spite of herself.

"Maybe that's why." He reached out to finger a lock of her short, dark hair. "Maybe how uncertain you are is what's driving it home for me—driving home how certain *I* am."

"Certain enough to bring me to a movie premiere, huh?"

When he gave another shrug in response, Davia moved close with intentions of putting a kiss to his cheek.

Kale turned to capture her mouth instead, his tongue thrusting deep the instant his lips touched hers. Her grip on the glass tightened and she feared the delicate stem might shatter in her hand. Her worries quickly faded as the kiss soon overruled all thought save the sensations coursing through her veins like sweet, warm syrup.

They shut out the room and everything in it. Soon the only thing existing for them was each other and the feel of their hearts pounding amid the strong, steady surges of their tongues battling in the grip of fierce emotion. Davia gasped sharply when she felt the proof of Kale's arousal against her. He felt it, too, and was breaking the kiss to put his forehead to hers.

"We should probably hit the road." His words were labored and he fought to calm his breathing. "My part in this thing is done. We're out of here tomorrow and I want as much time with you as I can have before then."

Davia pressed her nose against his cheek. "You're having time with me now," she murmured.

"Not for what I want to do with you. It's not nearly the right place for what I want to do with you."

"We could always stay here longer—in Miami."

Kale grinned over the tempting idea. "If only we didn't need to go back and get a decision so we know where we stand with that property. Besides," he added as he gave another tug to a lock of her clipped hair, "I need to get you back. You've got some thinking to do."

Davia's curiosity piqued momentarily but before she could ask what he meant, his eyes lit on her lips and all she felt was arousal. This time when he whispered that they needed to get out of there, she didn't hesitate.

Chapter 17

Kale and Davia were returning to Iowa before lunch the next day. Though the trip had been a quick one, both felt extremely rejuvenated and ready to tackle the challenges facing them.

Barry and Estelle weren't at the inn when they arrived. After a short call to Barry's cell, Kale discovered that the couple was tending to their other responsibilities—Estelle with her boutique and Barry with town council business. Still, the Waverlys were most interested to hear about the Miami trip. Barry had a special interest as he was a huge Xyler Chronicles fan. The couples decided to meet up at the town café for lunch.

Kale and Davia were seated in a booth, awaiting the Waverlys, when the sound of Davia's laughter reached him from her side of the table. "What is it?"

She was studying the street from the window next to their table. "I was just thinking what a difference a day makes," she said while she stirred her coffee. "From sun and fun to snow and relaxation."

"Relaxation?" Kale smiled curiously. "I thought that's what Miami was for."

"Seriously?" Davia ceased her stirring. "I don't know how you get *any* rest down there."

"You're one to talk." Kale laughed. "I bet you don't get much rest in the middle of San Francisco's hustle and bustle."

"I'd bet I get more than you do in Miami." Davia tempered her wager with a small grimace. "But less than I'd get here." She picked up her coffee mug and offered a small toast. "There's a peace to all this," she said as she studied the warm glow of indoor lighting that peeked past frosty shop windows along Main Street. "It's a peace you think about when you're home."

"So you're saying Mullins is growing on you?" Kale chuckled, returning to browse the folder he'd been studying at the table.

"You can't deny that this place hasn't appealed to something in you."

"Oh, you're right about that."

The look in his deep stare was easy to read and soon Davia had a fine idea of what had appealed to him the most.

"I really hope this plan of yours works, Kale," she was saying once their laughter had eased. "It'd be great to build something special here—something the people we love would be proud of."

Kale waited a beat and then dropped a thoughtful

look at the folder he'd been studying. "Do those people include Martella?"

Her nod was slow but firm. "Definitely yes. Tella, too. At this point, I think we owe it to her." A hint of resolve took control of her expression then. "I was thinking about what we talked about—me closing that private place where I was holding on to all the guilt I had about her."

Curiosity brightened Kale's expression.

"I'm ready to do that," Davia said.

Kale smiled. "I think she deserves it, don't you? So long as we never forget that she's too special to be completely removed from our thoughts."

Davia's nod became an enthusiastic one that she followed up with quick laughter. "I think she would've gotten a kick out of knowing we own a piece of land and that we were planning to build a movie theater on top of it. She always did love a good turn of irony."

"How ironic do you think she'd find this?" Kale opened the folder and turned the contents to her.

Davia leaned forward. It was another glossy photo of a theater. But this one sent her nostalgia rising and brought a poignant smile to her face.

"Tella…" Davia inched her fingers across the photo as she remembered her friend. She raised tear-sheened hazel eyes to Kale. "It's her theater."

Kale nodded, his expression carrying a similar poignancy. "It's one of a few shots I took when I visited for ideas. I guess I could've just printed images from the web site, but there was something about being there."

"Such a great place." Davia scanned the photo with unrelenting intent. "So you sold it back to her family."

He studied the photo and nodded. "My plan was to let some time pass and then sell it back to her. She knew I had no intention of keeping it and *I* knew she'd make it hard for me to return it, but I could see how much she loved it."

"I heard there's a row of art galleries there now."

"Better than a parking deck."

"So what's your plan?" Davia asked.

Kale shifted another look to the photo. "I think it speaks for itself."

Her lips parted in surprise. "You want to recreate Tella's theater here in Mullins?"

"Besides its original locale, can you think of anywhere else it'd be more at home?"

"Nowhere," Davia sighed.

The volume of voices in the café heightened noticeably and then someone was calling over to Kale and Davia.

"You two might want to get over to the town hall ASAP."

"Yeah, it sounds like Mitch Barns is on another one of his king-of-the-world rampages. He called an emergency meeting and everything."

Kale and Davia exchanged looks that were equally dismayed.

Groaning, Kale stood. "This can't be good."

It took quite a while to get the collected crowd settled that afternoon. As with the previous meeting, word had spread quickly about the primary topic on the day's agenda. Several shops along Main Street closed down as proprietors as well as their patrons made quick dashes for town hall.

Everyone wanted to claim a good seat for the fireworks that could always be expected when Mitchell Barns was on a rant. A great seat for impending drama, however, wasn't the only reason for the rowdiness of the crowd that afternoon.

Audience members were either huddled close where they sat or dispersed around the lofty room in groups of three or more. Excitedly, they chattered away with their heads angled in study of the photos they carried. Once Kale and Davia arrived, several made a point of stopping by to speak to them and to shake hands, while others waved from afar with their photos aloft. Photos of Mullins from back in the day. Photos of their family members.

"Looks like your idea was a hit." Davia smiled appreciatively at all the happy faces beaming inside the great hall.

Kale's handsome face was a picture of approval, as well, before it showed signs of trepidation when he gave a single nod toward the front of the room. "Looks like we're about to find out what the consequences of a good idea are."

Concern began to fray Davia's happiness, too, when she spotted the council members claiming their places at the front of the room. The twelve men and women all wore similar looks of unease. All, including Mitch Barns. The audience was still filing into their seats by the time Estelle found Kale and Davia and took the chair they'd saved for her.

"Do you know what this is about, Estelle?" Davia asked.

Estelle shook her head, her ebony stare wide with uncertainty. "No idea. No one's got any idea. The call for the meeting came from Mitch's secretary a couple of hours ago. Barry said the woman gave no details other than the time of the meeting."

"Wonder if there was something in those photos I sent to Sheila Barns that her husband didn't like."

Estelle sighed over Kale's concern. "Memories of the past can be a reawakening for some people. For others, they can be more painful than a root canal."

Kale began to stroke his jaw while considering Estelle's words. "People *do* like to lash out when they're in pain, don't they?"

Davia couldn't help but think of her own reactions to the past as of late. Fists clenching, she observed the group of grim-faced council members and tried to get a bead on their thoughts.

Council Chair Lucille Clancy stood behind the console and raised her hands to encourage order. She eventually resorted to a light bang of her gavel to gain the crowd's attention. Gradually the audience began to take notice that things were getting under way.

"Thank you, everyone, for coming to order." The councilwoman graced the crowd with a welcoming smile. "Things will be a little informal this afternoon as this isn't an official meeting. With that said, I'll turn the floor over to my fellow council member, Mr. Mitchell Barns, who has a few words to say. Mitch?"

Mitchell Barns made a slow push to his feet and nodded to his colleague. "Thank you, Madam Chair, for allowing this spur-of-the-moment gathering and thanks to my fellow council members for taking time out of your schedules to join me here today. I apologize for the mystery and I know you're all understandably confused about what's going on."

"Try edgy as hell," Estelle grumbled and then smiled when Davia reached over to squeeze her hand.

Mitchell Barns was fully turned toward his audience. "I know what your presence here is costing today. Many of you closed shop to attend. I also know that many of you brought along photos. I don't need to guess what's in them. Odds are they're similar to ones I have, ones of a time long passed—of people we know and love. Some who are still among us and others who have passed on but who still claim a place in our hearts.

"If those people are still among you," Mitch continued, "I would hope that everyone in this room would make a point of telling those special people how much they are loved. More than that, I hope you've all been told by those special people how much they love *you*.

"My father and I didn't trade i-love-yous regularly, but I knew I was loved. I thank God for closed doors, because my father could never say those words, much less show me any affection, when the world was watching. When his father was watching." Mitch silenced, giving the crowd time to murmur words of understanding.

"Many of you knew my grandpa Shep," he said, referring to Shepard Barns. "Many of you knew *of* him, knew his…points of view, his way of life, his crimes. Over the last several days, I've received photos, as you have. Photos of my father as a kid. Those of you who knew him may find it hard to see him as a kid. I did myself.

"He was a hard man—hardened over the years as I grew because my granddad said I'd never be worth carrying on the ideals of the family name if he didn't. My dad listened and, because of that, I grew up thinking he lost his ability to love anyone—even me. I did whatever it took to get his approval. Thinking, believing as he did, as his father taught him… It became a way of life for me, too.

"But this—" Mitch raised a glossy black-and-white photo "—this reminded me of the man I had the chance to glimpse before hatred and fear changed him. This photo and others I've seen—thanks to my colleague Bryant Waverly, his wife Estelle and our new visitors, Kale Asante and Davia Sands—have showed me and, I think, showed a great many of you, a time when our town was the true definition of family. A time when we didn't surrender to hate and fear. A time we'd maybe all like to see renewed.

"I called this meeting to say that any objections I may've had to moving forward with the proposal of a town theater have been tabled. I want to bring this back." Again he raised the picture. "This sense of family, of community, of welcome. Thank you."

Mitchell Barns reclaimed his seat while the hall remained silent. Seconds seemed to tick by and then there was a faint cry from the back of the crowded room.

"Way to go, Mitch!"

The room blossomed to life with cheers and roaring applause. Without his usual grandstanding, Mitchell Barns gave a soft smile and a single wave.

In the audience, Davia reached for Kale's hand and smiled when Estelle reached over to cover their clasped hands with her own.

Chapter 18

The Mullins town council unanimously approved the decision for the theater. Kale's premature meetings seemed to mature overnight. For the next few days he met with the various entities responsible for approving the kinds of licenses and permits required for the theater. Mitchell Barns's town hall speech had had a galvanizing effect on his fellow Mullinsers.

Excitement spread from one end of the county to the other in anticipation of the new entertainment venue that wouldn't be a reality for at least another two to three years. Though the craziness would quell, once the less exciting tasks of paperwork and other bureaucratic issues were under way, the elation showed no signs of dipping any time soon.

Mitchell Barns, humbled and modest during the

meeting with his colleagues and fellow residents earlier in the week, had reclaimed some of his more boisterous qualities. He announced a huge indoor winter barbeque at his estate on the other side of town. Everyone in town was invited and encouraged to bring guests.

Davia, having fallen in love with Estelle's boutique, tried to resist the urge to add more volume to her already overflowing suitcases. She wasn't certain of the dress code for such an event as the one Mitchell Barns had put on the town calendar, so when Estelle suggested another trip to her boutique—just to be on the safe side—Davia agreed it couldn't hurt. That day's visit saw the addition of two new sets of formal and casual wear to add to her growing wardrobe.

She was smiling approvingly at one of those new outfits in the mirror of her suite when she heard a familiar voice.

"I'm pretty sure Barry said jeans were fine."

Davia wasn't surprised when she turned to see Kale enter her room. They'd stopped locking their doors after their first night together. Still, finding him there leaning on the doorjamb, when they hadn't had much time to speak with one another since the unforgettable town meeting, shook Davia immeasurably. She was once again struck by his dark good looks, his virility.

Without realizing it, her fingers tightened around the shirt-collar bodice of the slinky black gown she'd been trying on.

"I decided to take Estelle's 'better safe than sorry' advice, but I already decided on jeans." She glanced toward the armchair near the alcove. There awaited a denim blazer with jeans and a walnut-colored cashmere sweater.

"Good choice." Kale smiled once he'd followed her gaze to the big chair. Soon, though, his eyes had returned to appraise her in the gown. "So where will you be causing men's eyes to pop out of their heads in that?" he asked as he walked toward her.

Davia glanced down at the garment that seemed to accentuate her curves. "San Francisco's got no shortage of events. I'm sure I'll find someplace to wear it."

"Does that mean you're going back soon?"

"Well, I— Of course." Her fingers slid from the dress collar. "We, um, we don't want to overstay our welcome, do we?" She tried her hand at teasing. "We've already cut into Barry and Estelle's finances enough, staying here for free as long as we have." He was almost close enough to touch her then and Davia felt her hormones jostling impatiently.

"We could just share a room," Kale said in a way that was both playful and serious. "Barry and Estelle could open half the floor so they could make a little dough, at least."

She couldn't stand it anymore and reached out to grasp the hem of the hooded sweatshirt Kale wore with matching pants.

"That sounds good to me." She brought him closer while linking her arms around his neck. She plied his earlobe with the faintest suckle.

"Davia—"

"Later." She kissed his mouth.

Kale didn't need much more persuading. In one swift motion he hoisted Davia against his chest then, shoving the recently purchased garments from the bed, he laid Davia there and followed her down. He consumed her mouth with the deep ragged thrusts of his tongue as his hand trailed up the length of her thigh, grabbing her gown and raising it higher to bare her skin.

Davia's unhappy moan filled the room when Kale brought an end to their kiss. She tried to pull him back to her, but he was kissing his way down her body and soon reached the juncture of her thighs.

He kissed her through the crotch of her panties, his arrogant smile igniting when she gasped at the sensation. Using his nose, he nudged aside the material and inhaled her scent before gliding the tip of his tongue along the seam of her sex. Davia's whimpering cries of approval were a thorough motivator and one he didn't ignore. He claimed her with one languid thrust of his tongue, which he held there for a heated moment.

When Davia squeezed her intimate muscles around his stiff tongue, Kale savored the act. He waited until it seemed she was on the verge of losing all control before he withdrew.

She held her patience in a frantic clutch and waited for him to continue. Instead, Kale raised up to cover her again and Davia eagerly arched into him. He dropped a kiss to her ear and she stiffened at the words he spoke against it.

"I apologize for this, Davia… I shouldn't be here."

"I want you here."

"Do you? Do you really, Davi? Or do you want to spend more time with this hot-and-cold dance we've been doing?" His rich chocolate stare roamed her face for a long moment and then he leaned close to put a kiss on her lips.

"Think about that," he murmured, moving back to give her a long sweep beneath his gaze. "That really is a great dress." Following the compliment, he walked out, leaving her alone.

"Estelle." Relief filled Davia's voice when she arrived in the kitchen just a bit out of breath late the next morning. "Have you seen Kale? I checked his room, but he wasn't there and I really need to talk to him."

She needed to tell him that he was right. She was just as curious to know where things could go between them as he was.

"Oh, honey." Estelle's expression relayed disappointment. "I'm sorry, but you missed him. He already checked out early this morning. I was up at dawn making him breakfast for the road."

"But...we've got Mitchell Barns's barbeque tonight." Bewilderment clouded her words.

"Yeah." Estelle nodded. "He said he had urgent business in Miami. He told me a jet would be on call for you whenever you're ready to leave. But it's okay. I mean, you guys are in business together now. You'll see him soon, right?"

"Right." Davia's voice went quiet but inside her thoughts raged explosively. Kale had effectively left the ball on her side of the court.

"Should we make up an excuse for you, too?" Estelle continued to work on the food she was prepping at the counter. She glanced back when there was no response forthcoming and laughed at Davia's curious expression. "We can make up an excuse if you want to go to Kale."

"Uh, no, no, that..." Trailing off, Davia tugged a hand through her hair and looked as though she were trying to get her bearings. "You don't need to do that. I mean...we're partners, like you said. We'll be seeing each other a lot from here on out."

"Mmm." Estelle gave the other woman the full benefit of her gaze. "If only this was about business, right?"

"Estelle..."

"What? I mean, I get the feeling all this is new for you and Kale. Like you just realized your feelings when you got here. Am I right?"

Davia hesitated on a nod and then gave in. "Yeah... yeah, pretty much." She took a seat at the kitchen table. "And I don't know whether to trust it. To trust myself. This whole thing...it just came out of nowhere, Estelle. There was no rhyme or reason to it."

"But you want to trust it, don't you?"

Davia couldn't summon a response.

Estelle didn't press for one. "When you've got your answer, let us know if we need to make an excuse for you tonight." Moving from the counter, Estelle squeezed Davia's shoulder on her way out of the kitchen.

Miami, Florida

"Sorry, guys." It was Kale's third apology since the start of the meeting that afternoon. He could barely keep his mind on the contents of the files in front of his eyes, let alone the discussion around the conference table. The words of his executive staff sounded like a monotonous buzz in his ears.

He could only think of Davia—the way she'd looked when he'd left her the night before. Flying back to Miami that morning, he'd asked himself why he'd left her. He told himself he knew why and then cursed himself for pushing her into a decision he had no right to demand of her.

No right to demand…and yet there he was back in Miami because…why? This was a meeting he just couldn't miss? The truth was he had only gone about making his demands a whole other way. Not by words but by action.

Kale emerged from his deep thoughts to hear his chief architect calling out to him. He smiled, not even trying to pretend he'd been paying attention.

"Guys, I guess I'm just not all there today," he said.

Several at the table began to chuckle.

"All there…that's a good one, K." His chief architect Lyle Neese grinned devilishly. "Sounds like your heart's still in Iowa."

More robust chuckling surrounded the table. Kale smirked, though his eyes held a look that was nothing short of pensive.

"Know what, Lyle?" Nodding, Kale stood. "I'd have to agree with you. Excuse me, fellas." He left his then silent conference room to make his way back to his office suite.

He stopped outside the cubicle of his assistant, Stephanie Merchant.

"Steph, I need you to contact Sully and let him know I need him back here ASAP."

Concern shadowed Stephanie's honey-complexioned face. "Everything okay?"

"No, everything is not okay." Kale's tone was harsh, but he shook his head upon noticing his executive assistant's concerned expression. "I need to go back to Iowa," he explained.

"Is there a problem there?"

"I hope not," Kale said, "but I did forget something."

Stephanie reached for the phone. "I hope it's nothing too important."

"Pretty important." Kale took a pen from the desk and began to twirl it idly around his fingers. "It's the woman I'm falling in love with."

Stephanie gasped, her fingers slowing on the keypad where she'd been dialing Kale's pilot Sullivan Cage. "Um, Kale, I don't think you're gonna need Sully for that."

Before Kale could ask Stephanie to explain, he heard his name—in Davia's voice. Turning, he found her standing in the entrance of his assistant's cubicle.

"Stephanie," Kale said without looking away from Davia.

"I know, clear everything for the day," Stephanie finished for her boss and then laughed when he sent her a pointed look over his shoulder. "Right. Clear everything until further notice."

Kale graced the woman with a quick smile, but uncertainty was controlling his features again by the time he looked back to Davia.

She took a short step forward. "Is there somewhere…?"

Kale was already nodding and extending his hand to urge her to follow him.

The grip of déjà vu held Kale as he and Davia made the short walk to his office. Kale recalled their first meeting little more than a month ago, which had begun in a similar fashion. As he had then, Kale once again smiled in appreciation of the subtle curves of her willowy body. That day she sported jeans and a wispy blouse and his approval was as high then as it had been the first time he'd laid eyes on her. More, as he now had proof of what she felt like in his hands.

In truth, little had changed between then and now. On that first day, she'd been a very beautiful woman he very much wanted to take to bed. Now, she was a very beautiful woman from whom he wanted so much more.

Davia slowed her steps when Kale moved closer to squeeze her elbow to guide her around the slight curve in the corridor. They were in sight of his office door.

Kale opened one of the double pine doors and waved Davia forward to precede him.

"Wow."

He heard her response before he closed the office door. He understood her reaction. "See something you like?" he asked anyway.

"Yeah, my office."

He laughed. "So did I when I saw yours."

The living area, with its astounding collection of books and DVDs, was beyond impressive. As was the mini gym in a far corner of the enormous room.

Davia hoped there would be a chance to talk about their mutual decorating interests at a later time. Just now she was interested in a different discussion topic. Walking into the room, she came to a stop in front of the built-in shelving.

"Did you mean it?" she asked while browsing the never-ending sea of DVDs. "What you just said out there?"

Kale didn't need a further reminder. "I meant it." He rested against the closed office door. "I should've said it before I left you in Iowa. Come to think of it, I never should have left you in Iowa. I was trying to…press my issue, to get what I wanted, and I'm sorry, Davia, for manipulating you that way."

She faced him then. "But, Kale, you didn't."

"You're here, aren't you?" His argument was soft yet pointed.

"I knew what I wanted long before you ever left." She let him see her sincerity and her unease. "It's not easy for me to admit to being afraid. Chances are there's still more of it that I'll need to deal with before all is said and done. I've only known three really brave women in my life—my mom, my aunt and Tella."

She let her gaze falter then. "Sadly, there were no instances of them having to prove their bravery in matters of the heart, so I had nothing to go on there. My aunt never married. Tella's theater consumed more of her heart than any man ever could, and my parents have a fairy tale of a marriage." She gave a mystified shrug.

"I have no clue how to be in a…relationship. I've never wanted a real one and it scares me that the one I want now is with a man I once disliked."

"Once?" he probed.

Davia lifted her gaze from the floor but still could not meet his eyes. "I'm not falling in love with you. I've already fallen, so if you're serious here, you've got some catching up to do."

Though a grin emerged, his words were firm. "It would probably scare you—even more—to know how serious I am."

She smiled, but her expression soon sobered. "We've got almost an entire country separating us, Kale."

"Is that part of what's scaring you?"

"Maybe…but I'd like to change that."

"Well, then—" Kale spread his hands "—I can't ask for more than that."

Davia reached for one of his extended hands. "I can." She tugged his jacket lapel and pulled him close to initiate their kiss.

The moment heated in the space of a millisecond. Kale wasted no time cupping Davia's neck in his hands as he took advantage of the moment to have his way with her mouth. His free hand had its way with the rest of her. It trailed beneath the hem of her blouse, one finger sliding along the inside waistband of her jeans. Then he was cupping her bottom, drawing her snugly against him. The kiss steadily intensified until Kale wrenched away from Davia, cursing as he did so.

"What?" She frowned.

Kale at first replied with a rather sheepish grin. "There're some things I don't keep on hand here at the office," he said.

She got his meaning. "That's a good thing to know."

"Not always."

"Well, that just lets me know that I should always be prepared with you."

Kale drew her against him then. "Nothing prepared me for you."

Davia smoothed her lips across his jaw. "Well, I think *that's* a very good thing to know."

"You're right." Somehow he gathered her even tighter. "That one's definitely good to know. Always." The word silenced on his lips as they claimed hers.

Chapter 19

Over the next several months Kale and Davia tried to make the distance work for them. It wasn't easy given the often rigorous demands of the responsibilities associated with their respective jobs. There weren't an abundance of complaints on that score, however. Being so busy left the couple with little time to fixate on the distance and grow scornful of its existence. Such was the case as far as Davia was concerned. It helped being back on familiar turf in San Francisco following the drama of Mullins and then Miami with Kale.

Kale kept himself just as busy. The Xyler Chronicles's premiere earlier in the year had provided his company with an unforeseen side benefit. While his multiplexes had been selected for many movie premieres over the years, they'd been smaller budget releases, though many of them had boasted rumors of major award nominations. There had been none of the big-budget blockbuster caliber, until Xyler. With that one came more offerings for premieres of such films.

The opportunities had been bittersweet. Sweet because they'd been additional jewels in the crown of his accomplishments. Sweet, too, because all the work had kept him busy and not in the position of having time to miss her too much.

The bitterness crept in when *not* missing her too much gave way to anger. Anger he directed toward himself—because of his decision not to assuage his impatience and go after what he wanted most. It was a decision he'd toyed with throwing over numerous times, especially in the last two months. Two months since he'd seen her! He was sure she was just as busy as he was. Aside from their own personal businesses was the formidable joint undertaking in connection with the Iowa theater.

Kale knew there would be plenty of time for them to devote to following up on the words they'd spoken to one another. So long as the decision he'd made didn't backfire. The decision he'd made to give her space and to leave the ball in her court. The possibility of that backfiring sparked a show of temper and he shoved a stack of papers from his desk.

"Go see her, why don't you?" Lyle Neese grumbled from where he stood hunched over a worktable on the other side of the office.

Kale didn't try denying that his loss of temper was about Davia. Lyle had been his sole sounding board for months. Ever since he'd started to regret the decision he thought he'd had to make, he'd been sharing his second thoughts with Lyle.

Kale bent to retrieve the papers. "I can't do that," he grumbled and pretended not to hear Lyle chuckling across the room in response.

"Would you care to explain how you reasoned that out?" Lyle asked amid his laughter. "She loves you, you love her. You've both said the words, right?"

Kale, still stooping near his desk, shook his head. "It's about more than that. I know she loves me, but she's dealing with more than that. This whole thing hit her out of nowhere," he continued. "For me, it was about meeting a woman who knocked me on my ass and showed me what I really wanted. For her, it's about not trusting herself." He smirked, renewed tension swelling inside him. "Since I've known her… I thought it was just me she didn't trust because of all the misunderstandings between us…but it's herself she doesn't trust."

"How so, man?" Kale had never shared that particular aspect, so his friend and employee needed clarification.

"She was wrong about what happened with Martella and me—and she wound up making a mess of things because of it. Then she figures the way she approached Martella's troubles was a wrong one and that misjudgment was worse given what happened to Martella. All that," he sighed, "plus the fact that she can never make it right. Not that she ever could have, but she can't see it that way."

Kale stood and dropped the papers onto his desk. "I pushed her enough, pushed her to listen—to accept the truth of what happened with me and Martella." He leaned against the desk.

"I pushed her to give me a chance when she was still trying to come to grips with that truth. Now, she loves me and I need to stop pushing until she's ready to accept more."

Lyle left his place at the worktable and walked over to clap his friend's shoulder. "Just don't forget that she's in California and you're in Florida."

"I got it." Kale's expression was a grim one. "But whatever happens now...it has to be her choice. It's the only way I can be sure she's faced that fear—the fear she has that her judgment's off and that any decision she makes is on shaky ground.

"She's got all she needs to move forward and believe her perceptions are on point, but *she's* got to be the one to take hold of what she's being offered, Lyle. Otherwise, she'll never be free of it and I'll never be sure she's really mine."

"She's the woman you love," Lyle said, "the one you want." He clapped Kale's shoulder again. "Just be sure you don't give her so much space that she loses sight of what she's being offered."

Lyle headed out of the office, leaving Kale with his thoughts.

San Francisco, California

Business concerns for Davia weren't an over-the-top matter when she returned to her San Francisco office. She had the utmost confidence in her staff and they hadn't disappointed her. There were a few jobs needing to be closed out, and she took care of them quickly.

The same couldn't be said for her brewery endeavors, however. Davia had never felt luckier to have her college friends and business partners on hand than she had over the months following her Iowa adventure. Success hadn't come without strings and as San Francisco Brews gained respect and name recognition, Davia and her partners found themselves in the midst of contract negotiations with local and franchised restaurants, supermarkets and pubs.

She was up to her eyeballs in brewery meetings that day, discussing with her partners their immediate and upcoming ventures.

"The Ayerses' pub tasting is a go but we've all yet to agree on a specific date." Jilly Tymes chewed on her pen cap while studying the big calendar that lay flat on the wide conference table. "And whether any of us should go along," Jilly tacked on as though it were an afterthought.

Davia smiled, not bothering to look up from the notes she'd been scribbling at the table. "Don't start, Jill," she sighed.

"What's the problem, Day?" Her other partner Audrey Graham wore an innocent expression that illuminated her round, lovely face. "I'm sure Jill only meant that it might be nice for one of us to attend seeing as how you already established the deal with your newfound friends."

"Oh, I see…" Davia finally looked up from her notes to fix Audrey with a smirk. "So this is all about business and nothing personal, huh?"

"Well, yeah." Audrey held on to her innocence and allowed playful curiosity to ease in alongside. "I mean, what could be personal about— Oh, right…you probably wouldn't get much work done with Kale there."

"You're right." Davia refused to take more of the bait. "We're in the middle of making final crew selections on the construction teams for the theater."

"Oh, yeah, the theater. I almost forgot about that part of the affair."

Davia rolled her eyes from Jill's smug smile and looked over at the only other partner at the table who had yet to speak. "Don't you have something to say— like 'shut up and get back to work'?"

Wilhelmina Owens offered an exaggerated shrug. "You know how I love to keep you guys in line, but it's kinda hard to do that when the truth is being spoken."

Davia held her head in her hands. "Not you, too," she groaned.

Jilly stood, still chewing her pen cap. "I know! Maybe we should all go. It's probably the only time we'll get to meet Mr. Kale Asante with Davia keeping him all to herself like she's been doing."

Davia pulled her head out of her hands. "I'm sorry, guys, I… I didn't realize."

"Time flies when you're having fun." Audrey snorted. "You know it *is* customary to introduce the fiancé to the family."

"Who said anything about a fiancé?" Davia hoped her expression wasn't as panic-stricken as the sound of her voice.

Wilhelmina laughed. "Hell, Day, you guys have been

together for about ten months now. You love the man, don't you?"

"Yes," Davia responded without hesitation and with no trace of panic.

"But…?" Wilhelmina prodded.

Davia hesitated then. "It's just…all been going so well, so…easy, and I…"

"Don't want that to change?" Jilly guessed.

Davia winced. "Am I selfish?"

"Maybe a little." Audrey reached out to pat her hand. "But don't be so hard on yourself. You're just trying to hold on to the new magic for as long as you can."

"New magic?" Davia pondered the phrase.

"At the beginning, you know?" Wilhelmina shrugged. "The time in the relationship when everything's still new and perfect. Neither can do wrong in the other's eyes."

"Right." Davia's sigh held a weary edge. "I think that part's over. I'm sure I've already crossed that line." She slumped back onto her chair. "We haven't seen each other in two months. The last few times we were together I got the feeling he wasn't too happy with me."

"Aw, girl." Audrey waved her hand again. "He probably said that because he thinks you're content with things the way they are and he wants more."

"And what if that's not it? What if he doesn't want more?"

"Davia, why would you think that?" Jilly asked.

"For one thing, he's in Miami." Again Davia moved forward to hold her head in her hands. "He's in Miami and he's…" She looked up to send a lazy smile toward her friends and business associates. "Kale Asante is only single because he wants to be."

"Well, from what you've told us and given all the time you guys have had together, I'd say Mr. Sexy and Single doesn't want to be alone anymore."

"You're right." Davia gave a mock salute to Wilhelmina. "He doesn't want that. I mean, he's waiting on me, isn't he? Waiting on me to make that move. Literally."

"One challenge at a time, girl," Audrey advised. "First, you need to make it clear that you're willing to do whatever it takes to be with him the way people in love are meant to be with each other."

Davia was still nodding her agreement when the conference phone line buzzed. "Yeah, Maggie?"

"Davia, Mr. Asante's here."

Momentarily speechless, Davia looked at her friends' faces. It was obvious she hadn't been expecting Kale, but before she could reply to her assistant's announcement, Wilhelmina was speaking.

"Maggie, this is Wil. We didn't even realize it was time for our meeting."

"What meeting?" Davia whispered.

"I thought we told you, Day," Jilly whispered back.

"Thanks. Maggie, could you send Mr. Asante in?" Audrey called.

Davia looked at them through narrowed eyes. "What are you guys up to?"

Jill shook her head. "I don't really think it's the time for explanations now, Day. Do you?" She was on her way to the conference room door, pulling it open before more could be said.

Kale moved into the room, his gaze immediately seeking out and locating Davia. His expression was guarded even as his eyes raked their way up and down her body. Then he was looking at Jill, whom he graced with a charming smile.

"Mr. Asante, please forgive us for using business to get you here." Jill took his hand in a warm shake. "If we'd waited on Day much longer for an introduction we'd have all keeled over from impatience. I'm Jillian Tymes, but everyone calls me Jilly."

"Nice to meet you, Jilly, and it's Kale, and there's no need for apologies. Your business idea was a good one. Wish I'd thought to reach out with it, but I've been a little distracted lately." Again Kale looked at Davia.

The other women in the room moved forward to introduce themselves while Davia hung back.

"Kale, would you excuse us for a minute?" Wilhelmina shared a quick smile with her partners. "We've been meeting all morning and I know I could use a break before we get started on this next part of the business."

"No problem, I'm not in a hurry." He looked briefly at Davia and then back to Wilhelmina. "Have you guys eaten? We could talk over lunch."

"Oh, Kale, that'd be great." Audrey took the liberty of accepting the invite while sharing the agreeing nods with her partners. All except Davia. She stood there, stunned.

"If you guys choose the place, we'll head out as soon as you get back," Kale suggested.

"I'm sorry about that," Davia finally said when her

partners left the room talking. "Sorry they put you on the spot that way."

"They didn't do anything wrong."

The bite to his words was undeniable to Davia. "Does that mean I have?" she asked.

"It doesn't," he reassured her and then shrugged. "I've just never been good with patience."

"Could've fooled me."

The shrug Kale offered barely sent a ripple through the fabric of the walnut-brown suit jacket that emphasized the striking chocolate depths of his stare. "Guess that means I've done a good job of hiding that flaw. Maybe I should try a little more honesty now."

Unable to formulate a quick comeback to his unexpected admission, Davia could only stand there and let her eyes do the talking. She'd missed him so. Two months and she'd almost gone insane with missing him. But she hadn't called and he was only there due to a ruse devised by her well-meaning business partners.

"I'm sorry that it took business to get you here. I should've called you."

Kale felt his jaw muscles clench and he bowed his head. "Would you stop apologizing to me?" He wanted to bridge the distance between them but resisted. "Did your partners tell you about the deal they want?" he asked instead.

Davia massaged the tense muscles bunched at her nape. "We never got past my surprise that they called you at all."

Kale broke into soft laughter. "A bunch of go-getters, huh?"

"I used to be one." Her tone was regretful. "Lately,

I don't seem to know which way is up." The apprehension squeezing her heart eased when she heard his laughter again.

"I know exactly what you mean," Kale said.

"Just give the check to me," Wilhelmina instructed the waiter once he'd recapped the lunch order.

"Very good, ma'am." The waiter gave a dutiful nod and then headed off.

"So, Kale, are you as in love with Iowa as Davia is?" Jilly was asking. "It's all she can talk about."

Audrey gave a short, happy laugh. "It's not *all* she talks about, Jilly."

"And for good reason," Wilhelmina tacked on.

Davia gritted her teeth while her friends traded sly looks and smiles. "Are you guys gonna wait till after we eat to get to the point of why you called Kale all the way out here?"

"Well, gosh, Day, we don't hear *him* complaining. Kale, do you have any complaints?" Audrey asked.

Kale's gaze was on Davia. "Not one," he said.

Davia was about to lose herself in the warm, deep pools. She managed to shake herself free of their spell. "Could we get to the point sometime before midnight?"

"Kale," Jilly sighed, shaking her head sorrowfully, "we should apologize for our partner. We'll see that she makes up for her rudeness later."

Davia bristled as Kale's laughter rang out.

"Anyway, Kale, we asked you out here to discuss your theater. We didn't say more before because we wanted to put it to you in person," Jilly explained. "We, uh…we figured the fact that we're in San Francisco would be enough to get you to take the meeting."

"Well, I could never resist a good mystery."

"Well, we won't keep you in suspense any longer." Wilhelmina scooted forward in her chair. "We'd like you to offer our brew in your theaters."

"You told me that much and I think it's a good idea. We've already got quite a few brews on the menu."

"How many have you got on tap?" Wilhelmina asked.

Interest simmered in Kale's eyes then. "We haven't gone that route yet."

"Is it a route you think you'd ever take?" Jilly asked.

Kale rubbed his jaw. "I don't see why not."

"We'd want exclusivity, Kale," Audrey said, "and placement at all your theaters for two years."

Kale whistled. "Go-getters with shrewd vision," he said to Davia.

"Well, we can't take all the credit." Wilhelmina looked to Davia then, too. "We only thought of it when Davia told us about the pub in Iowa—the possibility that they'd be interested in carrying the brew on tap. We couldn't realistically secure exclusivity at a bar or restaurant," she went on, "but for an out-of-the-box venue like a movie theater, our chances of securing something like that are much better."

"And since you're the only theater mogul we know who's practically family—" Jill's expression was playfully innocent as she let her statement hang "—we thought we'd give it a shot and bring the deal to you first."

"Excuse me." Davia pushed back her chair and left the table.

Audrey rolled her eyes in Jilly's direction. "You could've kept that part to yourself."

Jilly winced. "Sorry, Kale."

He was already waving a hand to dismiss any sleight. "Don't worry about it. You've got me interested. Put something in writing that I can take back to my people and we'll go from there." Kale spoke decidedly, but his gaze made a continuous shift toward Davia who was making her way to the back of the restaurant.

"Don't worry, Kale," Audrey said as she leaned over to squeeze his wrist. "We'll take care of business. You take care of our friend."

"That's all I want." His eyes were still on Davia. "Would you guys excuse me?" He didn't wait for a response and left the table.

"I like your friends."

Davia smiled when she heard Kale's voice behind her on the restaurant balcony. "So do I." She sighed and then snorted a laugh. "Despite their big noses that always seem to find their way into my business."

Kale smiled then, too. "I'm sure they mean well."

"Oh, I know they do. Doesn't make it any easier though—and it gives me no choice but to look into the mirror and be reminded of what a fool I'm being."

"How do you figure?"

Davia smirked at his question. "I believe you know. I'll even bet you guessed it while I was telling myself this was about me not stepping up to the plate with Tella when it was really about me being afraid of myself... of screwing up again. This time the lives at stake are mine and yours."

"You think that standing still ensures nothing changes—that no decisions have to be made?" He sounded certain of his guess.

"Half right." Davia turned and leaned against the balcony rail. "I thought I was…protecting myself by not making a decision, but things are definitely changing anyway." She gave him the full benefit of her gaze. "You were all right with this before—all right with the distance—but you aren't so okay with it anymore. That's changing us, isn't it?"

Kale moved closer then, not stopping until he was near enough to cup her face. "I love you." His thumbs brushed her high cheekbones as he smiled and shook his head. "That part's not changing."

Davia reached up to squeeze his wrist. "I love you, too." She moved to the toes of her riding boots and initiated a kiss.

"Prove it," Kale challenged when their kiss ended and he put distance back between them. "Marry me."

Chapter 20

Davia checked her watch for the third time since getting everything in place for the conference call she and Kale were scheduled to have with Barrett and Estelle Waverly. The call was supposed to have been a three-way from Iowa to San Francisco *and* Miami, but Kale's unexpected visit required a last-minute tweak of the chat logistics.

Kale had yet to arrive and Davia hoped that having the call at her place hadn't discouraged him from attending. She'd hoped he would've been early as she'd been walking around in a daze since the night before.

She'd heard that some men conjured all sorts of wildly creative ways to propose. Never had she heard of one popping the big question and then not sticking around to hear his intended's reply.

What was that about? She'd asked herself that question since Kale had turned on his heel and left her alone and devastated on that restaurant balcony. He hadn't made another stop by the table where they'd been having lunch with her partners. Instead, he'd instructed the waiter to charge him, not Wilhelmina, for whatever they ordered and then he'd taken his leave.

Her friends were understandably curious about what had been said between them, but Davia didn't know where to begin. With that being the case, she'd opted not to share any details.

Maybe he'd guessed she'd turned him down and had hightailed it out of there before he got his feelings hurt. Maybe he'd regretted ever asking the question at all.

The doorbell rang, successfully jerking Davia from her disruptive thoughts. Quickly she ordered herself to calm down and then went to answer it.

Kale waiting outside her door brought on a sense of déjà vu, sending Davia back to the first time she found him standing in her offices. It seemed like a lifetime had passed between them since that day. A lifetime hadn't passed, though. A lifetime was what he wanted from her now. She was opening her mouth to greet him, but he didn't give her the chance.

"Sorry I'm late," he said as he walked past her into the foyer. "Have you guys gotten started yet?"

Davia had to give herself a mental kick, lest she remain standing there speechless. "We, uh— You're not late. We still have a few minutes." She watched him interestedly, trying to get a bead on his mood, but he offered no clues. It was just as well, for the phone was ringing. Davia resented the relief springing to life inside her when the call interrupted her attempt. She greeted the Waverlys enthusiastically.

"How's the weather, guys?" Kale asked once he, too, had greeted the innkeepers. "Have you had the chance to meet with either of the crew chiefs or staff yet?"

"That's the, uh, main thing we wanted to talk to you guys about," Barrett confessed after a brief hesitation followed Kale's question.

Kale and Davia traded a look.

"Go on, B," Kale urged.

"Are you guys leaving it up to me and Este on who gets the final bid?"

Again, Kale looked to Davia, who nodded. "Well, uh, we were hoping you guys could act as the second opinions in this…"

"That's where I think we've got a problem," Barrett said. "See, me and Este…well, we kind of want both of the crews."

A third set of looks passed between Kale and Davia.

"We're sorry about this, guys." Estelle's voice chimed through the speaker. "We know you were looking to use our knowledge of the area to decide which crew would be the better fit."

"It's just that we think both teams have a great understanding and respect for what Lyle envisions in his plans. Though they're different understandings, we think they'd complement each other," Barrett noted.

"They're all getting along great and with two crews on the job we'd get all this done faster, right?" Estelle added.

"Estelle? Is everything okay?" Though the reasoning was sound, Davia couldn't help but feel concerned.

"Is there a reason for the urgency? Are folks starting to have second thoughts?"

"Oh, no, no!" the Waverlys chimed in at once.

"That's not it at all. On the contrary, actually," Barrett said. "Everyone's impatient to see it done, ready to enjoy a movie without having to drive almost forty miles to see it."

"We've come a long way." Kale sighed.

"So do you guys think a town's impatience for something it once fought diligently against is enough to justify the extra expense to have two crews on the job?"

Davia was already nodding in response to Barrett's query.

Kale grinned. "It's enough to justify it to us. We'll send word to our people and get things in motion for a move forward."

"So can we expect you two back for the groundbreaking ceremony?" Estelle asked with excitement in her voice. "It's sure to be quite the event. Mitch can't stop boasting. He's already planning the next big throwdown to celebrate all this getting under way after so many years."

"What? Does he already have the diamond-studded invitations made up?" Kale teased.

Barrett laughed. "Close!"

"So?" Estelle probed once the laughter had eased. "Can we expect you guys for the groundbreaking once a date's been set?"

"We'll be there," Kale promised.

"And, uh, will you be arriving together?"

"Este…" Barrett Waverly groaned his wife's name. Kale laughed, apparently taking the probe in stride.

"It's doubtful Davia will trust my pilot not to take her back to Miami." His playful tone belied the tension in his expression. "We'll be there as soon as you guys have a date."

"You'll have it ASAP," Barrett assured him.

The call ended and the Waverlys took whatever energy and excitement there'd been with them. Suddenly the room felt quiet.

"It was a good idea talking with them together," Kale finally said.

Davia nodded, pushing her house phone back to the corner of the coffee table. "Judging from where things stood not so long ago, I wouldn't have thought we could've hoped to put *one* construction crew in Mullins, let alone two."

Kale's smile was brief and then he was pushing to his feet. "I should get going."

"Can you stay for a while?" Davia stood, as well. "I thought we could talk."

Kale gave a slow shake of his head. "You know what, Davia? I'm about talked out."

"Kale—"

"And if this talk you want to have is about yesterday, forget it."

"Kale, please—"

"I'll stay, but not to talk."

Davia understood his intentions a second after he grabbed her. "Kale, wait—"

"I'm about all waited out, too." He crushed her mouth with his and began tearing her out of her clothes in the process.

Davia made a few valiant attempts to sway the approaching storm, but she quickly lost her desire to do so. Arousal peaked at a steady rate inside her until she had no care for talking or even for understanding the motives for his behavior the day before.

Kale had made it more than clear that he had no interest in talking. His hands were everywhere. Strong fingers gripped and tugged the fabric of her clothing, exposing her bare skin along the way. His mouth set ablaze the slender line of her neck, gliding lower until his tongue skimmed her collarbone.

Next, he was retracing the path to suckle her parted lips and then her earlobe. One he pampered with his mouth, the other with his fingers that massaged the plump, tender flesh. While he tended her lobe with his teeth and tongue, his fingers trailed down to explore the moist, dark depths of her mouth.

Desperately, Davia performed her own sensuous suckle of the digits plundering her mouth. The motion set her on fire and she pulled at his shirt. He had her half out of her clothes and she sought to render him into the same state.

Kale soon had Davia in his preferred spot hoisted high against his chest. With her so positioned, he buried his face between her lace-clad breasts to inhale the fresh, sweet scent of cucumber that infused her skin. He carried her to the sofa they'd shared for their business conversation. Now he needed its cushioned softness for more carnal endeavors.

With Davia straddling his lap, Kale began to feast on the nipples that were firming beneath the cream-toned bra cups.

Davia moved to shed the scrap of lingerie to bare

her chest to a more thorough exploration, but Kale prevented her efforts. He held her fast—a hand shackling her wrists and keeping them secure at the small of her back.

Kale was settled for a time, content in the pleasure her breasts provided him. Soon, though, he hungered for more and used the hand cupping her breast to ease around and undo the hooks of her bra.

Davia shuddered out her gratitude when she felt the air brushing her skin. Subconsciously, she arched her back, eager to have him at her breasts again.

Kale obliged. He released her wrists to cup and squeeze the dark, plump mounds. His mouth took possession of one as his thumb worked the ignored nipple into a more rigid nub.

Davia released unabashed sobs of delight into the room. Her hips undulated on Kale's lap, seeking an unnamed but obvious fulfillment. By then, she was clad only in a wisp of lacy fabric that matched her bra. The sheer material was no real barrier and she could feel him growing harder, longer, and insistently nudging the part of her in the direst need of his attention. With her hands freed, she tried her luck once more with taking him out of his clothes.

Kale seemed more open to the idea that time and allowed Davia to help him out of the denim shirt he'd worn outside of a pair of crisp, dark brown trousers. A white T-shirt showed beneath and it only took a few more seconds for her to drag it over his head once the shirt was a distant memory.

Hungrily, Davia let her nails scour the broad, rich caramel surface of his pecs and shoulders and abs. Her hips worked over his lap with greater intensity; she so wanted him inside her. She went to undo his pants, hoping he wouldn't stop her.

Kale had no plans to do any such thing. He'd reached his limit of resistance, as well. He wanted nothing more than to have the proof of that wanting clenched tightly inside her walls. Davia had already removed his belt and she was at work on the fastening and zipper of his pants. He remembered the protection he'd stuffed into a side pocket of the trousers and grabbed for it while Davia tugged them from his hips.

Their movements were a flurry of activity as they worked to fully relieve themselves of clothing. All the while, Davia maintained her spot astride Kale's lap.

Once he was naked, Kale expertly set the protection in place, even as he licked and sucked at Davia's breasts that were perfectly positioned in front of his face. Davia threaded shaking fingers through his hair. She was smoothing her cheek across the sleek curls crowning his head when Kale grasped her hips and settled her slowly onto his filling erection.

Davia's moans transformed into rhythmic gasps that kept time to the tempo Kale set as he lifted her and lowered her to accept and release him. When her gasps took form and she was able to speak his name, he kissed her appreciatively. It seemed he was still in no mood to hear anything remotely resembling conversation.

Davia wasn't complaining. Weakly, she moaned while taking his deep and branding kiss. Kale halted the kiss to return his focus to her breasts. Soon, he was back to favoring them with an intense array of sensual assaults that targeted the glistening, pebbled nipples.

Their moans hit the air in simultaneous, heated fashion. Kale cradled her ass in his palms, squeezing and cupping the globes as he lifted and settled her to his delight, his tempo increasing, faster and more powerful until he took them both to the pinnacle. The moment was explosive, echoing with shudders and groans. The climax pummeled them both, ebbing and flowing through them in endless waves.

It seemed hours had passed. The only sounds were their heavily labored breaths. Then Kale finally moved. He gathered Davia in his arms and took her up from the sofa. He didn't put her down until he'd carried her up the winding staircase to tuck them into the first bedroom he could find.

"Yes."

Kale was leaving the bed to go hunt down his clothes, hours later, when he heard her. Davia said nothing more but he knew she understood there was no need for more words. His heart beat so wildly against his ribs that he wondered whether she could hear it, and issued silent orders for the muscle to cool it. He grimaced then, taking stock of where they were.

"It's the sex talking," he said.

"You know that's not true."

"Do I, Davia?" He partly turned to her. "Do I really?"

She averted her gaze to the tangle of linens and pillows strewed across her bed. "You've got every right to be pissed." Silently, she acknowledged the fact that she'd let her own anxieties and fears bring them to a point where the words of love they'd shared had given way to insecurity. Shaking off what was, Davia focused on what she wanted to be. "You'd have known it wasn't the sex talking if you'd let me give you an answer yesterday. Why didn't you stick around to hear it?"

"Maybe I was afraid of what I'd hear."

Surprise robbed her of speech for several moments. "You thought I'd say no? Just no and that's it? Even after I told you I love you? Did you not believe me then?"

Kale turned his deep stare toward the tangled linens, as well. "I believed you at first because it was what I wanted to hear." He ran a hand over his head in a jerky, frustrated manner.

"Then, I began to think your reason for saying it may've been because you weren't ready to give up what we shared." Again, he cast a meaningful look upon the bed.

Davia wanted to touch him, but she reconsidered. Instead, she sat up, keeping the sheet tucked beneath her arms as she moved. "Given where we are right now, I know it's hard for you to believe this, but when I told you I was *falling* in love with you, I meant it. When I told you I loved you, I meant that, too.

"I love you, Kale. I love you despite the fact that a serious relationship wasn't even on my radar and then… there it was as big as day and with you, of all people—a man I'd despised, misjudged. It was a lot to deal with especially when…other things came into play." She cast another of her pointed looks to the bed then, too.

"You were right when you said I was…standing still, hoping that would keep things from changing. I'd gotten past all that and didn't want to do anything else that might…rock the boat. Outside of my parents' marriage, other relationships have always seemed so complicated—ones I've seen from the outside looking in. I think that's partly why I shied away from my own. But this…us… It's been ten months of bliss, much more than I ever thought I'd be capable of."

"Because you didn't trust yourself."

Her smile confirmed his guess. "I already told you I was stepping out on a limb with no kind of expertise to guide me in this sort of thing. The last two months I know you've left the ball in my court." She shook her head and seemed to bristle. "I didn't want to do anything that would mess that up."

"You wouldn't have," he swore.

Davia didn't look convinced. "When you distanced yourself…I thought maybe I had, but you were just trying to give me time to figure out what I wanted. To take the leap in making a decision. To believe I had the ability to make a good one. I get that now. It didn't help at first. I spent a lot of time second-guessing every move…still obsessing over whether I was even worthy of a relationship with you after the way I misjudged you.

"All that…" She sighed. "It clouded things, kept me from seeing as clearly what you were able to so easily."

Kale shifted, only allowing her to see his profile then. "I guess my final push with the proposal didn't help things, either, did it?"

She smiled. "You knew what you wanted. I couldn't fault you for that."

"And you?" He faced her fully. "Is this what you want, Davi?"

She scooted a little closer to him. "Between the two of us, I think I was the first to have my thoughts head in this direction. You said once that I surprised you. You surprised me, too. I think I knew a future with you was what I wanted before I could even admit it. I think that's why I could never let go of the fact that it was *you* I was feeling this for. That part I just couldn't wrap my head around even after I knew the truth, even after you forgave me for labeling you the way I did. I want you, Kale. I want a life with you more than I want to give any more of my energy to the past—real or imagined."

Her smile was one that spoke of helplessness. "I know there's a lot more I could say—a lot more I should say. I just hope you can believe that now, here, where it's just the two of us—no town hall meetings and crisis, no meddlesome but well-meaning friends, no distance."

"No distance." Kale's voice was firm as he echoed her words. He took her hand, squeezed, kissed it. "Will you marry me, Davia Sands?"

She squeezed his hand, clutched it hard. "In case you have thoughts on running before you hear my answer." She scooted closer. "Yes, yes, Kale, yes." Her gaze was long and unwavering as it searched his.

"Yes, yes..." she continued even as he kissed her.

"So will we be Kale and Davia Asante of San Francisco, California or Kale and Davia Asante of Miami, Florida?" he asked once he released her mouth.

Davia linked her arms around his neck when he set her to his lap. "Gosh, I can't seem to think past the Kale and Davia Asante part. But if you need an answer right away, I do believe that I'm old-fashioned enough to let my husband decide on our mailing address."

"Are you sure?" He spoke the question against her temple.

"You can run your business from anywhere," Davia said. "So can I... Hmm, maybe this distance issue isn't nearly as big of a deal as we were making it out to be. Not nearly as big of a deal as us belonging to each other."

"I love you," Kale said.

"I love you." Davia hugged him to her and said, "Wherever we call home."

Epilogue

Mullins, Iowa
Two and half years later

"Asante Sands," Davia announced as she stood looking out at the dazzling marquee that towered in the center of a newly paved parking lot. If the night played out as all the others had over the course of their opening week, the theater would be almost filled to capacity when it opened later.

She smiled, feeling Kale's arms sliding around her waist when he moved behind her.

"No second thoughts, I hope? I didn't think you'd mind the name," he said.

"Oh, no." Davia rubbed the back of his hand. "It sounds like a destination. I think it's got a nice ring to it."

"So do a lot of things." Kale gnawed her ear and then lifted her hand. He kissed the ring adorning his wife's finger.

Davia turned in her husband's arms before she looked up to survey the lobby, washed in golden light by a never-ending sky of recessed spotlights occupying the theater's ceiling. Next, she observed the eye-catching design of the carpet—a sea of navy diamonds in the center of a rich purple base. The diamonds were outlined in white with the design set against a black background. The artwork repeated across every square inch of the theater's flooring.

The irresistible and unmistakable aroma of popcorn permeated the air and drew the eye to the wooden concession stand that had the look and allure of a turn-of-the-century pub.

"Do you think they'd approve?" Davia leaned into Kale's chest and sighed.

He smiled, knowing she was referring to their lost loved ones. "I believe they would." His voice was soft with reverence.

Arm in arm, the newlyweds made their way through the lobby and into one of the four theaters the establishment boasted. Each of the venues held the look of a cozy living room—one that could seat up to fifty-two people. Instead of labeling the four venues by number, each bore the name of those who had inspired it. The Chase. The Bryant. The Gloria. The Tella.

"Think we could do this again?" Kale asked when they entered the Tella theater and he pulled Davia back against him.

"Hmm." Feigning skepticism, Davia studied the

room's cozy old-world beauty. "I'm not sure. We had a lot of motivation for this one."

"You're right." Kale pressed his face into the back of Davia's head, enjoying the fragrance clinging to her cropped cut. "But I kind of like working with my wife."

"Well, there're a lot of perks," Davia said as she gave a quick, saucy shrug, "but it'd be a little difficult. I'm still handling business out of San Francisco while you're in Miami."

The couple had yet to decide where they wanted to put down stakes. They had divided their time equally on opposing coasts over the eight, blissful months of their marriage.

"I've been thinking a lot about that, you know. Where we handle our business." Kale entertained himself by rubbing a spot along her nape. "I kind of like the office space here," he said.

Davia turned, speechless and clueless until growing awareness brightened her eyes. "Are you serious?" She laughed when he only looked at her. "I didn't think a place like this would be your cup of tea."

Kale brushed his nose along her temple. "Guess I found a flavor I like. Can you say the same?"

Davia slapped his shoulder. "You know I love it here! But—I mean, it's so quiet." Faint uneasiness narrowed her light eyes. "Won't you go a little crazy? You won't find the same things here that are in Miami."

"Damn straight. I didn't find you in Miami, remember? I found you here. I'm afraid that's kind of sold me on the place."

"Well…technically you found me in San Francisco," she teased as excitement kindled in her tummy.

Kale gave a noncommittal shrug. "I never would've come to San Francisco if it hadn't been for this place."

Davia closed her eyes and nodded. "It would seem you've exhausted all my arguments."

"Finally." Kale looked up as if to offer thanks. "So do you think we'll work as well together building our house as we did on this theater?"

"Well, husband of mine, houses are different. There's more to consider and I may find myself having to convince you of things in my own sweet way, of course."

"I'm sold," Kale murmured seconds before they were losing themselves in a lusty kiss.

The moment was interrupted by the sound of a throat clearing. Ending their kiss, Kale and Davia saw their young theater manager, Alan Crump, on the other side of the viewing room.

"Sorry for the interruption, Mr. and Mrs. Asante. Just doing my walk-through."

"It's okay, Alan, you're just the guy I wanted to see." Kale took Davia's hand and pulled her a brief distance behind him. "How long till our first showing?"

"Just over three hours, sir."

"Sounds good. I'm trying to convince my wife of something and I need help setting the mood."

"Yes, sir." Alan seemed eager to assist.

"Thought we'd check out something on-screen," Kale told the young man.

"Yes, sir. Any preferences?"

"None, as long as the lights are down, Alan," Kale said.

Alan chuckled. "Not a problem, sir. We've got a new love story that just opened this week."

Kale gave a wave. "That'll work."

Alan left while his employers selected their seats and moved the cushioned rolling armchairs closer.

Kale, preferring to share a seat, pulled Davia into his lap. "Think this'll be a good movie?" He nodded toward the screen as the lights went down.

"Good." Davia got comfortable on her husband's lap and then sighed. "Not spectacular, though. I think that label should be reserved for our love story."

Kale nuzzled the soft spot behind his wife's ear and kissed her there. "I think you're right," he whispered as the movie began.

* * * * *

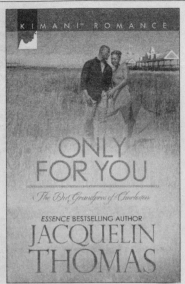

REQUEST YOUR FREE BOOKS!

2 FREE NOVELS
PLUS 2 *FREE GIFTS!*

KIMANI™ ROMANCE

Love's ultimate destination!

KROM15

The porch light flickered, casting the area in shadows. She'd been meaning to change that bulb.

"Thanks again," she said, getting her keys out of her purse.

Jacobe took her elbow in his hand and turned her to face him. He stood so close that she had to tilt her head even farther back to meet his gaze. In the flickering light of the porch, she couldn't make out the expression in his eyes.

"I respect your honesty, Danielle." His other hand came up to brush across her chin. "Don't think this kiss means otherwise."

Her heart fluttered and anticipation tingled every inch of skin on her body. "Who said you could kiss me?"

His dark eyes met hers and the corners of his mouth tilted up in a sexy smile. "Tell me I can't and I won't."

The air crackled around them. Sparks of heat filled her chest. Her eyes lowered to his lips. Full and soft. Based on the smoldering heat in his eyes, his lips desperately wanted to touch hers.

"One kiss," she whispered.

Don't miss FULL COURT SEDUCTION
by Synithia Williams, available February 2017
wherever Harlequin® Kimani Romance™
books and ebooks are sold.